MW00880225

Dance For Me

By Helena Newbury

© Copyright Helena Newbury 2013

The right of Helena Newbury to be identified as the author of this work has been asserted by her in accordance with the Copyright, Design and Patents Act 1988

All characters, events, entities and places in this book, other than those clearly in the public domain, are fictitious or are fictitiously used, and any resemblance to any real persons, living or dead, or real places or entities is purely coincidental.

Front cover photo: Casara / istockphoto
Rear cover photo: istockphoto / Thinkstock

ISBN-10: 1490402713

ISBN-13: 978-1490402710

DEDICATION

To S - you know who you are.
With thanks to my beta readers Andra, Ava, Julianne
and Nadia and my editor Liz.

Helena Newbury

CHAPTER ONE

Natasha

I CRASHED THROUGH THE MAIN DOORS and had to stop dead as a gaggle of actors rushed across in front of me. For a second, my back cooked in the New York sunshine while my front froze in the icy chill of the old building. As soon as I could, I snaked past the actors and ran up the stairs.

Second floor, and I was blocked by a musician coaxing a massive, sticker-covered keyboard case through the door of a practice room. I considered climbing over him. I was in that much of a hurry.

I slipped past him and bounded up the next flight of stairs, my bag knocking against my back. I was going fast, but not *too* fast. The stairs at the academy were concrete, topped with black and white linoleum that was there before man walked on the moon. Every dancer knew the story of Sabrina, who missed her footing and went ass-first down half a flight, breaking her femur and missing an audition. That wasn't going to happen to me. *Not today*.

Third floor and a few dancers were already milling around, ready for class. The class I was about to be late for.

My normal routine was to arrive early and get it done before anyone was around, but the bar I worked at hadn't shut until 2 a.m. and I'd slept straight through my alarm. My choices were clear: get to class on time, but skip the only thing that would calm me; or head to the restroom, do it and face Miss Kay's wrath.

It wasn't really a choice. I could already feel the first tendrils of panic winding their way around my chest, tightening and tightening until they could yank me suddenly down.

I ran to the restroom and stuck my head around the door. Every one of the stalls was empty. I sprinted down the room and flung myself into the last stall in the line, ramming down my jeans and sitting all in one movement.

I pulled the vintage cigarette case from my bag, running my fingers over the embossed metal. When I bought it, it had stunk of tobacco so I'd rubbed Ylang-Ylang oil all over the inside. Pretty soon, the smell of Ylang-Ylang was hardwired in my brain to cutting. When I opened the case, the waft of it calmed me a little all on its own.

An alcohol wipe first, freezing and clammy on my inner thigh.

People thought we were suicidal, or at least foolhardy, but I was actually very careful. The last thing I wanted was a trip to the emergency room with some doctor peering at my legs. I took out a razor blade—I always used them fresh from the box—and wiped it down with another alcohol wipe, just to be on the safe side.

High up on my left inner thigh, there were six thin slashes of red, ordered by age from left to right. By the time I ran out of room, the oldest one would have healed. I was methodical like that.

I took a deep breath and started to cut.

People thought it was about the pain. I mean, they didn't think that about *me*, because no one except Clarissa knew. But when they read about some poor girl in a magazine article, they shook their heads pityingly and thought that, if she wasn't suicidal, she must be some sort of pain junkie. Not me.

When I was under stress, I felt myself...sliding. Like the floor under my feet had tilted and my whole life was shifting out of control, too fast for me to do anything about it. The memory of what happened when I was fifteen was there, the guilt waiting with open jaws as I slithered and skittered towards it.

Cutting gave me an anchor. When I cut, I immediately felt like I was latched in place, and the feeling lasted the rest of the day—sometimes into the next one. From that toehold, I could tentatively stretch out and reach other things, like friends and rehearsals and sitting eating lunch around other people, without falling to my doom. My daily dose of punishment—a millionth of what I deserved—offered up as some sort of appeasement, to stop the guilt swallowing me whole.

The day loomed before me—rehearsal followed by a trip across town followed by the biggest audition of my life—and it was like staring down the side of the Hoover Dam. I could already feel myself falling, spinning and screaming towards—

The blade traced a vibrant, scarlet line across my skin, and it was like slamming an ice axe into my slippery life. I panted and dangled there for a second, then cut a little further, just to be sure.

I slapped an alcohol wipe over the red line and clamped my lips together as it burned. Then I peeled a dressing off its backing and slapped it in place. I knew from experience that it wouldn't show under my tights. I wrapped the blade in each of the used wipes in turn—I didn't want some poor janitor to lose a finger—and dropped it in the bin. I checked myself in the mirror before I ran for the locker room. I was normal, for another twenty-four hours.

***

I ran into the rehearsal room late enough to get a solid glower from Miss Kay. Another five seconds and it would have been the full rant. I'd only endured that once in all the time I'd been at the academy, my freshman year, and I could still remember it word for word.

"Miss Liss!" She always did that, used "Mr." and "Miss". It made you feel like you were about twelve. "Do you believe I roll out of bed each morning with the primary aim of speaking to my goddamn self? Do you believe I exist as an automaton, teaching dance to the walls and you happen to be in the room by happy accident? Do you want to have any *hope—whatsoever— of getting a dancing job that doesn't involve someone poking a dollar bill into your garter?"*

Every eye was on me. "No, ma'am."

"Would you like to switch? Is that what it is? Do you want an easier life? Do you want to go join the musicians downstairs and sit in a dress playing the cello on a goddamn padded stool? Do you want to transfer to acting and stare in the mirror trying to find your fucking motivation?"

"No, ma'am."

"Then do me the courtesy of showing up to my class on time!"

The glower I got was tame by comparison. I liked

to think Miss Kay had warmed to me a little, after two years, but I was probably kidding myself.

I grabbed a tennis ball from my bag and put it between my ankles, then started doing some gentle rises at the barre. A second later, I saw Clarissa's reflection move in next to mine in the mirror.

Clarissa had been my best friend since I'd arrived at the academy. We'd met at the door on the first day of our first semester. Fresh off the bus from New Hampshire, everything I had in a faded red rucksack as big as I was, I'd stood in front of the doors looking up at the old brick building. Clarissa had stepped out of a cab in a grey Prada dress, long blonde hair laser-straight down her back, and wheeled over her glossy black suitcase. We had nothing in common, but for a second we didn't even have to speak. We just looked up at where we'd be spending almost every waking moment of the next four years and our shared fear bonded us for life.

Clarissa was from Boston and had as much money as I didn't. When we'd rented a place together, everyone argued over who was dumber—her for moving into a dive with me or me for moving into somewhere I couldn't afford. It had actually worked out great. If I hadn't had the upward pressure from her, I would have wound up in one of those neighborhoods where crime scene tape litters the sidewalks. And if Clarissa minded not living in some fancy Upper West Side loft, she never gave any sign. I had a feeling she quite liked slumming it.

"Nervous?" She looked at me as we rose and sank in time.

I gave her a mournful look. The audition was easily the biggest thing I'd done.

"It's ballet. You'll ace it."

Ballet was easily my strongest style, as well as my favorite. Of course, I was never going to be in a top ballet company—no Fenbrook dancer was. Ballet dancers apprentice with a company when they're sixteen, when I was still in a foster home. They're on contract within six months and their careers are over when they're thirty.

Fenbrook gave us a slightly different path. We went in when we were eighteen and studied dance—or music, or acting, or some mixture of the three—and came out four years later with, in theory, a lot of practical experience and skills that would give us options after our bodies burned out. It was a good plan, but now that I was past the midway point, I was starting to panic. I was twenty-one and if I didn't kick-start my career soon, I wasn't going to have one.

***

By the end of the morning, I'd done two hours of ballet and one hour of modern. I was tired, but in that warm, loose way that comes from exercise. I took a shower, put on a fresh outfit under my street clothes—so I could avoid changing at the audition and keep my scars hidden—and hit the streets.

The audition was across town and I could have taken the subway the whole way, but I needed carbs and walking the first few blocks took me past a bagel stand. Two raisin and cinnamon bagels cleared out my loose change. It was going to be tight until I got my pay from the bar, and most of that was going to disappear on rent.

I'd worked my way through one bagel by the time I reached the subway station. As usual, Andy was sitting on a blanket outside, holding his "Veteran" sign and getting the occasional dime from passers-by.

I'd met Andy my first week in New York. He'd helped me figure out the subway map and ever since, he'd been like a good luck charm. He'd told me, over scalding hot coffee from Krispy Kreme, about fighting in Iraq. He'd been barely older than me, when he first returned. I'd tried to keep him fed through the bad times—when he barely recognized me, his eyes wild from missing his meds—and the good times, like now.

"I'm helping out at the soup kitchen," he told me proudly as he ate the bagel I gave him. "Two nights a week. If I can get a good word from them, I figure I got a shot at something in a restaurant or a bar. Hell, even washing plates. Then maybe move into the kitchen. Get rid of this thing." He tapped the Veteran sign.

I'd been leaning against the wall of the station, but now I slid down and sat next to him. "Really?" That sign almost seemed like a part of him. I'd watched it go through about seventy iterations, the cardboard more like cloth, it had been folded and unfolded so many times, the front of it festooned with little hand drawn Stars & Stripes and laminated with Saran wrap.

He shrugged. "I've seen enough vets wither up and die. You got to hang on to your past, but if you let it own you, it'll kill you."

***

After that morning's crazed rush, I made sure I arrived early for the audition, warming up in the corridor until they opened the doors. I checked out the competition: some younger than me, a few a little older. Sixteen of us in total. The woman from the ad agency told us it was for four parts.

The commercial would be for some anti-anxiety med, and they wanted to show some women prancing their way through their daily lives—at the office, at home, commuting—with "their lives made joyous and free" (she actually said that) thanks to the wonder drug.

They'd apparently got some hotshot director to film it, so the whole thing would be high budget and glossy. Exactly the sort of exposure I needed.

There'd be set choreography for the actual ad, but for the audition they were going to just play a couple of pieces and see what we did. I got the impression they wanted to weed out the actors who could dance and keep the dancers who could act. Except I wasn't either. I was a dancer, plain and simple. For the seventeen thousandth time that semester, I cursed myself for not taking a single acting class. There were only a handful of us "pure" dancers at Fenbrook, and I was beginning to see why.

The studio had been soaking up the sun through its large windows all morning, and someone hadn't cranked the air conditioning up high enough because it was uncomfortably warm. None of us wanted to be the one to complain, though, so we just toughed it out.

They were calling us in surname order, which put me midway through. Each dancer would get up from where they were lounging against the wall, walk into the middle of the studio and do the part while a group of suits from the ad agency and one woman I'd pegged as the choreographer watched. One dancer bugged out—just grabbed her bag and ran for the door after she'd seen the first two dance, realizing she was out of her depth.

As I watched the others, a faint sliver of hope just peeked over the horizon. I wasn't anywhere near the standard needed for the New York ballet, but then they didn't have time to audition for some commercial. The teaching at Fenbrook—ferocious Miss Kay included—put me in the top tier. I'd danced to the first piece plenty of times before and could remember the choreography I'd learned. The second one was deliberately obscure. I'd have to ad lib it, but so would everyone else. I could do this. All I had to do was avoid a mistake.

My turn.

I walked to the center of the room and bowed my head. As the music started, I sank into a demi-plié and powered upwards, turning and flowing through a sequence of steps and building towards a grand jeté. I pushed off and *flew*, that glorious rush as my feet left the floor, one leg forward and one back as I floated. I heard a little intake of breath from the choreographer. I was off to a great start. I was going to—

There was a noise like a thunderclap. I landed heavily, my concentration destroyed. Time seemed to slow down, and as my ankles complained at cushioning my messy descent, I looked towards the back of the room. A lock of hair had slipped loose, and I was brushing it from my eye when I first saw him.

He was still moving. He must have barreled through the doors and now he was trying to brake, one foot out in front of him. Soft, black curls were bouncing and flopping over his forehead and his mouth was slightly open, as if he was gasping—*at what?* Then my eyes locked on his, drawn in as if by a magnet, and once on them I couldn't look away.

Whenever I panicked and started to think about what happened, I felt myself start to slide. Nothing seemed solid, and I had to cling on to something real so I didn't wind up a bawling mess of tears on the floor. The cutting was my anchor, my one solid thing. Suddenly, looking into his eyes, I could feel myself start to slide. But it wasn't the familiar downward rush, the feeling that the room had tipped under my feet. It was the opposite.

I was rising, instead of falling, and felt...*connected*. This guy, this stranger, was the solidest person I'd ever met. It was as if he was lifting me up to safety from the cliff face I'd been clinging to.

Everything else seemed to fade down, as if the lights had dimmed. All that existed were those eyes, achingly blue and so honest and clear that they seemed to go on forever, like looking out to sea. I wanted to keep looking at them forever.

They say that you can see emotion in people's eyes, but I'd never really understood what they meant until that moment. As his lips parted farther, I could see the shock turn to fear—the realization that he'd done something horribly wrong. He managed to stop his forward rush, and the shirt he wore flapped and moved as if in a breeze. The thin fabric molded against his pecs, his broad chest like a wall. I started to realize how tall he was, easily a half-head taller than I was.

The music stopped and time restarted.

The choreographer turned and glared at the guy and then nodded to some chairs at the back, where a couple of dancers' friends were waiting. He moved over to them, but his eyes didn't leave me once. What the hell was going on? Why was he looking at *me?*

"Sorry," the choreographer told me, even though it wasn't her fault. "Let's go again." She cued up the music.

I returned to center. I was physically shaking, both from the shock of stopping so suddenly and what was rushing through my mind. I felt weak, almost light-headed and the air burned in my lungs. Where there should have been calm and serenity and the next few steps, there was a swirling, hot wind with him at its core. I glanced at him. He was sitting down, the smooth muscles of his arms bunching and flexing under his shirt as he moved. Then his eyes were straight back on me, watching expectantly.

"Ready?" the choreographer said, her finger

hovering over the button.

I nodded, but I wasn't—not even close. I was frazzled and off-balance and scared. He was in my mind, pushing everything else out of the way. I'd never felt anything like it before. I couldn't dance.

He was easily the hottest guy I'd ever seen. And he'd just made me blow the biggest audition of my life.

CHAPTER TWO

Darrell
Twelve hours earlier

BLAZING SPARK ARCED OFF THE WELD and hit my bare forearm. I jumped back and cursed, but my words were barely audible over the pounding music and that took all the satisfaction out of it. I ripped off the welding mask and slammed down the welding torch, then kicked the waste paper basket across the room for good measure. The night was not going well.

I stretched my back as I walked down to the other end of the workshop. I'd been hauling around hunks of metal and bending them into shape all evening and now I was starting to ache. I stared at the equations on the whiteboards, as if I could will them to give me a different answer, but they were starkly clear in their dismissal. I could work away welding the casing all I liked, but I was avoiding the real problem. I still had no way of making the damn thing fly the way it needed to.

I looked at the prototype missile, eight feet long and six months in the making. I'd done everything I'd set out to do, except get it to dodge—change direction, mid-flight, to avoid anything trying to intercept it.

I had a relationship with my work. Some would have called it a dysfunctional one—even an abusive one—but it had worked for me, for the last four years. Each project consumed me, but it also fed me, giving me the energy to keep going. The trick was to finish the project before it ate me up completely. This one was already a month overdue, and there was no end in sight. The project was winning.

I'd planned on it being a late one—maybe even an all-nighter. One of the advantages of having no boss is being able to set your own hours, and I often worked pretty weird ones, into the early hours and then sleeping until lunch—if I slept at all. But raw effort wasn't going to fix this problem.

What I needed was inspiration.

I killed the music, and the workshop went quiet as a tomb. Three floors underground, there was no traffic noise, no birdsong, no nothing. Within seconds, the silence was driving me crazy. Memories started floating up to fill the void—things I didn't want to think about.

I popped the top on a Dr. Pepper, fell into a chair and switched the big desk monitor from a blueprint to the TV cable feed. Movies I'd seen before. News I already knew. A documentary on Bigfoot. I went through my usual channels and headed into deep, uncharted cable territory. Food channels. Home makeover channels. Art—

A freeze frame of a ballerina hanging in mid-air. No, she wasn't frozen, she was moving—just moving so gracefully it looked like she was floating at the top of her jump. My thumb hovered over the button, ready to move on, but something stopped me.

She landed, twirled—what did they call that, a pirouette?—and took off again, energy coming from nowhere. I sat forward, transfixed. I'd only known ballet in a very abstract way: fat kids in pink tutus falling over and old rich couples dressed up in dinner jackets and gowns, paying hundreds of dollars a ticket. I'd never actually watched it before.

The dancer took a single step forward and then *tipped* and I actually rose up out of my chair, horrified, thinking she was going to fall flat on her face. But she hung there, balanced on tiptoe—no, not even tiptoe, her foot was actually straight, up on the end of its toes! How the...?

She seemed to lie there in the air, as easily as a bird floats on a thermal, and then the idiot who'd edited the program together cut to another shot and I lost her.

I sat there staring at the after-image of the dancer in my mind, one hand running through my hair, and something kicked into gear, deep in my brain. A tiny, tantalizing glimmer—a feeling that this was important. I always trusted that feeling. Inspiration can come from weird places, sometimes—I once solved a navigation problem after reading something about humpback whales.

I wanted more. I hit YouTube and started watching clips from ballets around the world, devouring them like snack food. By 4 a.m. I realized I didn't really understand what I was looking at, so I hit Wikipedia and learned about history and styles, which lead me on to composers and choreographers. I immersed myself in ballet, swimming in pas de chat and port de bras.

6 a.m. I sat down and watched *The Nutcracker* end to end, then made coffee and watched *Giselle*. By lunchtime, I'd worked my way through *La Sylphide* and

some of *La Bayadère*. My head was filling up with moves and shapes. I could feel my brain twisting and realigning, preparing to come at the problem from a new direction— it was working, even if I didn't know where the hell this was all leading me. I needed to share it with someone so, as always, I called Neil.

Neil's like my big brother. He took me under his wing at MIT and we kept in touch after I dropped out and he graduated. I could hear traffic roaring past. He must be out on his bike, stopped by the side of the highway to take the call.

"Mm-hmm?" said Neil.

"Did you know they go through a pair of shoes in a performance?" I blurted out.

"Who does what?"

"Their hip flexors have to rotate out 90 degrees. Can you imagine that? Their legs have to turn *sideways!*"

"Have you been up all night again?" I heard a horn and what sounded like a semi truck blast past him. I could imagine Neil nonchalantly lounging on the saddle of his Harley, barely off the road. It was impossible to faze him, which was probably why we got on so well. I knew I could come over a little...intense.

"Where can I see some ballet? Live, in person?"

"Um...I don't know...some place in the city? Like, don't they have a building for it?"

I was checking websites as I talked to him. "They're all *tonight*. I need it now."

"It's *vital* that you see some ballet *right this second?*" He didn't sound all that surprised by this. He knew the way my brain worked. "I guess there are rehearsals, and auditions and things? Maybe you could get into one of those?"

I was already typing. Deep in the bowels of a dance website, I found a listing for an audition starting in an hour. "I found one! Gotta go!"

**

I had a cold shower to make sure I was fully awake, but I didn't need it. Despite the all-nighter, I was more fired up than I'd been in months, desperate to follow this thing through. I knew that inspiration could be as transient as it was powerful. If I didn't chase this thing down it was liable to slip away from me and I'd be back to kicking the waste paper basket.

I had no idea what the hell you were meant to wear to a dance audition—especially one you were crashing—so I pulled on jeans and a shirt. For a second, as the shirt went on, I glimpsed the scars on my side, the sight of them hauling up the memories from the dark depths of my mind, screams rising in my ears.

My hands clenched into fists. *Focus. Finish the project. Move onto the next.*

I took the elevator up to the garage, grabbed my helmet and swung my leg over my bike. It was easier when I was working, the memories pushed back by the intense concentration and blocked out by machine noise, or music, or both. When I rode, my only distractions were weaving through traffic and the sound of the engine.

Which is why I'd bought a very powerful bike.

I flipped my visor down and cranked the throttle on the Ducatti. I was doing fifty before I'd left the driveway.

**

I begrudged every moment away from the workshop. Finding my inspiration was essential, but why did getting there have to involve so much wasted time? The thirty seconds I spent waiting at a Stop sign nearly drove me insane. Someone once told me that sharks have to keep swimming, or they die. I could relate.

I parked the bike on the sidewalk. I knew I'd get a ticket, but the thought barely registered, the cost negligible next to the money the missile would bring in. I started jogging towards the dance studio and then broke into a run. I couldn't help it. I could feel the call of inspiration dragging me in even as the pressure of the project pushed me forward. Inside, I could hear classical music coming from upstairs, so I sprinted up them two at a time, crashed through some double doors and—

She was frozen there in mid-air, like the dancer on TV who'd started all this. Except that dancer hadn't had soft, long lashes, eyes half-closed as her arms stretched gracefully above her. She hadn't had cheekbones that led my eyes down to her lips, pursed in careful concentration. Her beauty didn't just make me stop, it damn near floored me. I skidded to a halt and stood there like an idiot, just inside the doors.

Everybody in the room turned to look at me, which is when it hit me that maybe I should have inched the doors open quietly.

The dancer's eyes flew open and she landed, her poise thrown off by my clumsiness. I felt like I'd just shot down a bird. I'd never been the most sensitive person, but right then even I realized I'd messed up. All the energy I'd felt as I'd charged through the city and up the stairs drained away, leaving a sickening, tight knot in my stomach.

A fierce-looking woman nodded me to a chair and I slunk over to it, but I couldn't take my eyes off the dancer as she struggled to recover. All that was going through my head was *please be okay*.

CHAPTER THREE

Natasha

*F*OCUS, NATASHA. YOU CAN DO THIS. *You're a good dancer. You're the best.*

Every affirmation and confidence booster I'd ever learned was spooling through my head on fast forward, and none of them were working.

The music started and I sank into my plié, but it was mistimed and awkward. Immediately, my mind was shrieking at me. *I've messed up, I've messed up!*

Concentrate. Push into the jeté. Float. *Just like when I saw him.*

Distracted, I wasn't ready for the landing and slipped a little. There was a sound from the watching dancers, that tiny, sympathetic intake of breath you never want to hear. The room was suddenly the size of a cathedral, every pair of eyes like a spotlight on me.

Three easy turns came next, time to get my mind straight. But coming up was a fast-moving combination and I wasn't focused. I was drunk on his eyes and his chest and that feeling he'd given me, for once in my life, of being grounded, of having something to cling onto that wasn't cutting. I was a mess. I shouldn't have been driving a damn car, let alone trying to dance.

I've messed it up. The best chance of my life and I've wasted it.

Maybe because I thought it didn't matter anymore, I glanced across at him. He was still staring straight at me, his chest rising and falling under his shirt. He'd been running. That's why he'd crashed through the doors—he'd run all the way up here. *Why?* He didn't look like a ballet fan.

And then I got mad. I hadn't messed up. *He* had. And I was damned if I was going to throw this away.

I went into the pas de bourrée, three quick steps on pointe and my legs felt steady and firm, the anger lending me strength. I sank into a plié and then, as I came up, one leg whipped out to propel me into a turn. Again. Again. Every time I spun around to the front my eyes met his, and the anger grew and grew. It was about more than just him and messing up the audition, now. It was my past and my present and my future, my whole goddamn life, right back to when I was fifteen—

I pushed that from my mind with the next leap, leaving my thoughts behind and letting the raw heat of the anger carry me, no more than a puppet in its grasp. The problem with letting the feelings out was that once started, they couldn't be stopped. I flowed through the final few steps knowing I was too fast, too out of control. I had to get a hold of myself.

The music ended and the next piece—the obscure one—began. I hadn't heard it before that day, but I'd listened to it again and again as the dancers before me had danced to it and I was getting to know it pretty well. It was soft and romantic, calling for lots of slow, sweeping moves, as if an unseen lover's hands were carrying me. I knew exactly what it needed, but I didn't have a hope of pulling it off, feeling the way I did. I wanted to scream and kick, not swoon and float. What the hell did I know about romance, anyway? It had been a year since anyone had even kissed me.

My eyes closed for a second. I was on the point of walking out. The anger that had powered me had dissipated and now there was nothing except—

His eyes, staring straight into me—

I let myself flow into an arabesque. It was crazy because no guy would ever want—

Thick muscle bulging under his shirt as he'd sat down—

Not me. Jasmine or Karen or Clarissa, but he wouldn't want fucked up, twisted me—

Those lips...what would they feel like if he—

And suddenly I was turning around an invisible *him*, imagining his thumbs stroking my cheeks as his eyes blazed into me, our lips about to meet.

What the hell is this?

It was insane, but it was all I had.

Just go with it!

On my next pirouette, I imagined him kissing my neck...my breasts. The feelings were as strong as the anger had been, every nerve in my body taut and trembling with the sensations. When I turned towards him again our eyes met, and now it wasn't anger I could feel building. Time seemed to slow, allowing me to make my movements graceful and controlled. When my leg extended in a développé, I could almost feel his large, warm palms sliding down my calf. When I arched my back, it was as if I was leaning into him, my head on his shoulder and his breath on my neck. The music was only suggesting the steps. I was dancing to something

21

altogether more mysterious and dangerous, something I'd never felt before. I couldn't take my eyes off him.

And then the music ended and I sank into a demi plié to finish. I should have been grateful that it was over, that I'd survived it. But right then, staring across the room at him, I didn't want it to end.

I was suddenly aware that the room was deathly silent. I mentally shook myself. What the hell had *that* been?

The suits from the ad agency were glancing at one another, as if no one wanted to be the first to speak. Eventually the choreographer said, "Yes. Thank you."

She sounded more shell-shocked than dismissive, but shell-shocked couldn't be good. I knew I'd messed up the first piece, my anger showing through. I had no idea about the second one. It had barely felt like me dancing.

They were going to let us know at the end which of us they wanted back for a second audition, so we all had to wait around. I sat against the wall, taking sips of water and taking surreptitious glances at the mystery man. The man who'd messed up my audition. The man I couldn't stop thinking about.

Clearly, he'd come here to watch the dancing. So why, whenever I looked up, did I see him still looking over at me?

***

When the last dancer had finished, the three suits and the choreographer went into a huddle and exchanged scribbled notes. There was some nodding, and then the choreographer stood up. Clearly the suits, while happy to spend their day ogling women in leotards, weren't brave enough to risk the wrath of a slighted dancer.

"Thank you all for coming. I'd like these four dancers to come forward to talk about a second audition."

My heart launched itself up into my throat and I felt as if I was sliding again. I felt for the calming memory of the fresh cuts...but weirdly, I found myself looking to the back of the room. Searching for those cool blue eyes, wanting suddenly to cling onto him, instead.

He wasn't there. He'd slipped out while I'd been looking at the choreographer.

I listened as she read out four names. Mine wasn't one of them.

I grabbed my bag and ran.

CHAPTER FOUR

Natasha

I PUSHED OPEN THE DOOR TO THE STREET and let the draft of air cool my prickling eyes. *Don't cry don't cry don't cry—*

"Don't cry." A voice so deep I felt it as much as heard it. There was so much earnest empathy in it—as if by crying I would hurt him as much as myself.

I spun around. He was standing right outside the door, those crystal-clear eyes right on me. Something surged up inside and stole my breath. It had been two minutes and I felt like I hadn't seen him in months. *What the hell?*

"Hi." He sounded confident, but with just a hint of hesitation. Because he knew he'd messed up my audition, or because he'd felt what I'd felt? Both?

I realized I was standing there with my mouth open, and snapped it shut. "Were you waiting for me?"

He looked at the door. "I thought you might get swept past me, inside. This is a bottleneck." As if that

25

was a perfectly reasonable explanation.

"I didn't get the part," I told him stupidly. I should have been angry with him—should have slapped him across the face and raged at him. But all the anger seemed to have disappeared, as insubstantial as smoke in the face of what had followed.

"I'm sorry. Dance for me."

I thought I'd misheard. "...what?"

He stepped forward, and the breeze blew his shirt against his body, the arches of his pecs showing through the soft fabric. His clothes looked expensive, but he didn't look like the suits from the audition. Out here, with the wind playing through his hair, he looked like some demi-god, standing on a mountaintop. He was so much taller than me, with a big, looming presence that spoke of hard, manual work. I could imagine him wielding a sword, or forging one.

"Dance for me," he said again.

Oh my God! Was he some ballet company bigwig from another city? Or another director, stealing dancers from someone else's audition? He didn't look old enough to be either, only three or four years older than me. "Who are you?"

"Darrell. Carner."

"I meant more...what's your connection with dancing?"

"I need inspiration." He stepped a little closer, right into my personal space, and his hand went out as if to touch my face. He stopped just short, as if he knew that would be a mistake.

My heart beat faster, and not through fear. I wanted his hand there, wanted to know how it felt against my cheek. "What do you...do?"

He was staring right into my eyes. "I'm an—" And I saw his expression flicker, just for a second. "An engineer—an inventor. I need a muse."

I must have frowned, because he continued.

"I'll pay you. By the hour."

That snapped me back to reality. What was this? Was he trying to pick me up? *Me?* A guy like *this?* Ridiculous. So this must be something weird, possibly even dangerous. "No."

"But—"

I walked away, cutting him off, and with each step away from him, I tried to convince myself I was doing the right thing. No guy—especially no guy who looked like him—was going to try to pick me up. But even if it had been some sort of pick-up line, I'd avoided something messy and complicated. What would have happened, once he saw through the façade and got to know the real me?

And if he really had wanted me to dance for him one-on-one—well, that sounded creepy, right?

Only weirdly, it hadn't, coming from him. It had sounded heartfelt and genuine, like he really *did* want a muse, like some renaissance painter. But what did an engineer want with a muse?

I slowed my pace as I let the possibility trickle through. What if he'd been for real? What if this guy who'd seemed more *solid* than anyone I'd ever met, really had wanted something as simple as to see me dance again. And I'd turned him down....

I spun around, but he was gone. I stood there, jostled by passers-by, and felt my stomach sink. I had the awful sense that I'd just been presented with something special, and had lost it forever.

Well, fine. It was no more than I deserved.

***

Our apartment block looked worse than it was. Someone had layered shiny black paint over the outside walls in an effort to cover up the cracks, making it look like a glistening, rotten tooth. We figured it made the rent cheaper, though, and when we were inside, we didn't have to look at it.

I slunk in through the main door and listened. I could hear six-shooters and horses from one floor up and my heart sank. That meant Mr. Kresinski was sitting there with the door open, as he always did when rent day drew close. I really didn't feel like facing him, but unless I wanted to crash out in the hall, I didn't have much choice.

Kresinski was Polish, and ran the whole apartment block himself since his wife died. He was about seventy, with a thick white beard, and looked like a sad-eyed Santa. It wasn't that he shouted at us, or threatened us, or tried to get into our pants. It was far worse than that. He laid on the guilt.

"Natasha!" he called out as he saw my head rise above the handrail. "Natasha, how did the audition go?"

I'd told him a week ago and, of course, he'd remembered. "I didn't get it."

"Ohhh!" He looked so sorry for me that I wanted to hug him. "They are all idiots, Natasha," he told me, his voice shaking with outrage. "All idiots! You dance like an angel!"

"Thank you, Mr. Kresinski."

"I'm so lucky to have you and Clarissa. I hear tales from other landlords of people your age: they do drugs, they have the police round, doors are broken down, they don't pay their rent—" He made that noise that only Jewish people over sixty can do convincingly, like "*Oosh!*" He looked at me somberly. "But I can always rely on you, Natasha. Thank you."

I smiled a sickly grin and nodded as I walked up to our floor.

Inside, I leaned back against the door and sighed. I liked the door to our apartment. It was a huge heavy thing that must presumably have been made of wood, but felt more like lead. Whenever I closed it, I felt like I was snugly isolated from the outside world.

I was doing the math in my head. Three days to go until payday—it would be noodles until then. Then my bank balance would leap into the black for one delirious day until the rent hammered it back down into the red again. I wasn't sure how I was going to get through the rest of the month. *Is it meant to be this hard?*

"Clarissa?" I waited for her reply, then remembered she was rehearsing that night. She'd landed a part in some tiny off-Broadway show and they were scrambling to get ready for when they opened in a week. I was on my own for the evening. *Damn.* I tried to avoid time alone. The last thing I needed was space to think.

I felt a shift, like the floor had slid under my feet a few inches and left me closer to the edge of the cliff. I knew what was waiting for me at the bottom, if I let myself fall off. I had to *do* something.

I fired up the TV and turned the volume up loud, then flicked desperately through the channels. I watched heartbreak and tears, elegant heroines and cigar-chomping heroes, and none of it worked.

I got up and cooked: pasta, garlic mushrooms, bruschetta...far more food than I needed or wanted. I ate a plateful of pasta and wrapped up the rest for Clarissa, then cleared everything away. Then I cleaned the kitchen, scrubbing at the sink until it shone, even mopping the floor. But I still felt like I was sliding closer and closer to that cliff edge, with nothing to cling onto.

I sat down on the slippery tiles, panting. I had to

stop this fast or I was going to have a full-on meltdown and Clarissa would find me stretched out on the floor in hysterical tears. I couldn't let that happen. I'd held it together for over a year and I wasn't going to slip now.

My bag was in my room, twenty steps away. Nestling in it, the cigarette case and its pack of perfect, shining blades.

No. There was another way.

I stalked through to my room and stripped off my clothes, throwing on some old shorts and a worn t-shirt. Then I went over to the bike.

I'd bought the exercise bike when I moved to New York and realized I couldn't afford a gym. I'd scoured Craigslist until I found exactly what I was looking for, a fifty-something businessman who'd bought one to get in shape and then come to his senses. That had two advantages: he'd bought a top of the line model that wouldn't wear out any time soon, and he let me have it for a bargain price because he was embarrassed and wanted to get rid of it fast. We hauled it home in Clarissa's car and two guys from the academy (both of them ultra-helpful in the hopes of getting into Clarissa's pants) manhandled it upstairs for me. It took up a good portion of my by-no-means-huge bedroom and was too heavy to push into the corner when I wasn't using it, so it had to be permanently in the way, right in the middle of the floor.

People had said I was crazy—why not just ride an actual bike instead of the subway, and get my exercise that way? They didn't understand what I needed it for.

I climbed on, the feel of the saddle calming me just like the Ylang-Ylang scent of the cigarette case. I started to grind my way through the initial resistance, like running through oatmeal. As I fought past the inertia, my legs started a steady rhythm and my speed picked up. Lights flashed excitedly on the screen, telling me how well I was doing, but I didn't care about them.

I focused on my feet, kicking them down on the pedals as if I was trying to launch myself into orbit. My speed rose, so I notched up the resistance, the bike's hum rising in pitch. After a few minutes, my legs were warm and I could hear my breathing. Good.

I leaned forward over the handlebars, speeding up again, my legs like pistons trapped in an endless cycle. My body was just an engine to power them. I could feel the burn starting in my muscles, my thighs and hamstrings beginning to complain. Good.

I was gritting my teeth, sweat running freely down my back. The air was hot in my lungs, my muscles screaming, my heart hammering on my ribs like it was going to burst clear out of my chest, but it was worth it. Because with every turn of the pedals, I could feel my world growing more solid, more real, the sweat under my fingers and the fire in my legs evidence that I was *here* and not back in that house in New England.

My legs pumped faster, my upper body rigid. I had my head down, hair covering my face. I notched the resistance up to maximum, gasping for breath, out of control. I wasn't a person. I was a *thing,* a piece of meat tortured by the bike and I deserved every—

I stopped pedaling, my legs going limp. The momentum of the pedals dragged them around and around for minutes afterwards. Sweat ran in rivulets down my cheeks, as if I was crying.

When I finally dragged myself off the bike, my limbs were like dully-throbbing lumps of lead. I left a trail of soaked clothes as I stripped off on the way to the bathroom. Just before I climbed into the shower, I caught a look at myself in the mirror.

The sweat had made the mascara run in long,

black lines down my cheeks and my body was clammy and trembling. Strands of hair were plastered to my forehead and neck. How could he—how could *anyone*—possibly be interested in me?

I got under the shower and cranked the ancient lever over to freezing. Icy water cascaded over me, stealing my breath, but even as I shivered and gasped, it seemed to cement me in the present.

When I'd got so cold I didn't really feel it anymore, I turned off the shower and wrapped myself in one of the threadbare towels. Semi-dry, I padded back to my room and found my old bathrobe—the one a boyfriend brought me back from Vegas, with the hotel name on it. I curled up on the couch in the lounge, no longer panicky. At last, I could actually think about things.

Things like Darrell.

Who was he? Some guy who liked ballet? He sure didn't seem like the type. Ballet fans tended to be well-off and mostly older. His clothes had been expensive but *he* didn't look rich. Rich guys, in my mind, sat behind desks all day running companies or trading stocks and shares. Darrell looked more like a construction worker, or a fire-fighter—something physical. He looked like he worked his ass off.

I cuddled into the robe a little tighter. I had a pretty good memory, and I had no trouble bringing up a nice, clear image of his face, the locks of black hair falling down over his forehead. He'd looked like he might be Irish, with those big, blue eyes. And when he'd sat down, his shirt pulling tight and the collar open just enough...I closed my eyes and in mind, I traced the line of his collarbone down, following it across his body and over the smooth rise of his chest. I tried to imagine what he looked like under the shirt. If I just...inched...it up.... I knew his stomach was nice and flat, so I gave him a strong, defined six-pack. I could almost feel them under my fingers, thick bars of muscle under soft, perfect skin. Was he an inny or an outy? Definitely an inny.

I shifted in the chair, eyes still closed. My hands slid around his waist and upwards, pushing the shirt up with them. I'd glimpsed a strong back, when he'd turned to go to his seat. My palms slid over his muscles, my imagination filling in the gaps. I was very close to him, close enough that I could feel the heat of his body.

I imagined sliding my hands down to his ass. Blue denim, tight over firm cheeks, maybe a little intake of breath from him as he felt my hands there. I pulled him close and, rubbing up against me, I could feel—

Someone cleared their throat.

My eyes flew open.

Clarissa was standing there in the doorway—she must have crept in, thinking I might already be asleep. She was staring at me, mouth open, trying to find the words.

I glanced down at myself, puzzled. I was blushing a little at what had been going through my head, but it wasn't like Clarissa was psychic. My robe hadn't fallen open or anything, so why did she look so shocked? I just looked like I'd fallen asleep sitting on the couch, one arm across me and one—

OhmyGod!

My other hand was between my thighs. I must have slipped it there, about the time my hands reached Darrell's ass.

My face bloomed with heat and my own mouth fell open. We just stared at each other for a moment, and then I whipped my hand away as if it had never been there. "Hi!" I said loudly, in the hope that would make her forget what she'd just seen.

Clarissa gave me a look, but didn't push it. I had a

feeling that moment was going to come back to haunt me. "How did the audition go?"

I'd been trying to avoid thinking about it. Not only had I met easily the hottest guy I'd ever seen and walked away from him, I'd also blown my big break. I shook my head.

Clarissa pulled me up off the couch and into a hug. "What do we say when we don't get an audition?"

"I'm a useless dancer and I'm never going to get a job?"

She swatted my ass.

"Um...A door that's closed...is just an opportunity disguised as a glass half full?"

She swatted my ass again.

"They're morons. Where's the vodka?"

"Attagirl!" And she headed for the kitchen.

All of us—dancers, musicians, actors—had rituals for when things didn't go well. You had to have a way of dealing with it, and it couldn't be going out on a three day bender (or eating a tub of ice cream) because we wouldn't be able to function. It had to be a moderated release. Hence the ceremonial vodka shot.

Clarissa returned with two shot glasses and a bottle of vodka so violently orange it hurt my eyes. Clarissa had tried Skittles vodka at some party and I'd had the idea of making it using only the orange ones, extracting every one from about ten packs. We stored it in the freezer, so it was ice cold and syrupy.

"They're morons," Clarissa reminded me by way of a toast, and we clinked and drank. Orange sugar slid down my throat and then a second later the burn of the alcohol kicked in. I felt a little better.

"Anything else happen?" Clarissa's eyes flicked to the couch. She might as well have asked, "Who were you thinking about?"

The whole thing was enough of a mess, without bringing anyone else into it. Besides, I was never going to see him again. I shook my head. "Nothing. There's food in the refrigerator."

I headed to bed before she could argue. And I dreamed.

CHAPTER FIVE

Darrell

THIS WAS GOING TO BE A PROBLEM.

Ever since seeing her there, hanging weightless in mid-air, I'd been able to think of nothing else. I'd gone looking for a muse and I'd damn well found one. That overwhelming feeling I'd had when I'd first chanced across the ballerina on TV, that there was something *important* about dance—had come back when I'd seen her, stronger than ever. She was what I needed.

What I hadn't been ready for was *her*. The way her lips pursed in concentration, the way her hair shimmered and gleamed when it was pulled back into its severe dancer's bun—save for that one, gorgeous lock that fell across her face. Her body, elegant yet curvy compared to the other dancers I'd seen, the firm swell of her breasts making me catch my breath when she arched her back just so....

I wanted her, more powerfully than I'd ever

wanted a woman. And I was never going to see her again. I had absolutely no way of contacting her—even if I could get her to change her mind.

I slapped my hand over my eyes as I remembered what I'd said. Who says they're an *engineer*, even if it's true? Why hadn't I told her I had money, or a big house, or—

I knew why. I didn't want someone who was interested in the money. I'd tried a few of the high society parties, mostly because Neil wanted to try his luck with the women. I'd put on the suit and stood around with a glass of champagne and pretended to be interested in trust funds and venture capital. And yes, some of the women had been beautiful and I'd even tried dating a few of them, but we'd broken up within months. We just had nothing in common. They were all *rich*. I was just a guy who built stuff, who happened to have wound up with money.

I needed someone more like me, someone who did something with a passion. She was perfect...and I'd let her walk away.

I hadn't slept the night before, and eventually fell into bed around midnight, asleep before I could even pull my clothes off.

***

The next day, I got up early, made a pot of really serious coffee and *thought*.

Should I search for another dancer? It wouldn't be hard to find someone who *would* dance for money, right here in my house. But now I'd seen her, I didn't want another dancer.

I sighed. I had to give it up. She was one person in a city of eight million.

I stood up and paced, eventually winding up next to the half-finished prototype. Back to work, then. Forget about being happy, or having a normal life. Back to making a better, faster, more efficient way of killing people.

My knuckles turned white on the handle of the coffee mug and a voice inside me said, "*No.*"

I turned my back on the prototype and sat down at my computer. I had Google and Facebook and the dance websites I found the night before. I knew her rough age and I could make some assumptions—like she was probably in some sort of dance school. String all that together and I was looking at thousands, not millions. And although I might not know her name, her face was burned into my memory forever.

Of course, if she wasn't from New York—if she'd flown or driven in from out of state to go to that audition—then it was all over. But you don't solve problems by worrying about *ifs*.

I got to work.

Two hours later, I had a program that would grab the photo of anyone on Facebook between 19 and 22 (I'd pegged her at 21, but I couldn't be sure) who went to one of the long list of dance schools, academies and colleges I'd drawn up. It eliminated the men and then flashed up the photos one every second on my monitor. I poured more coffee and clicked *Go*. The hell with the odds. I was going to find her.

Helena Newbury

CHAPTER SIX

Natasha

I N HIGH SCHOOL, ENDLESS DANCE rehearsals kept me way too busy for a boyfriend.

Freshman year at Fenbrook—my first week, in fact—I hooked up with a sophomore actor. He was playing the lead in some crazy post-apocalyptic version of Hamlet and that made him a superstar to wide-eyed little me. Three dates and we were rolling around on the bed in his apartment. Four dates and I was no longer a virgin. Fifth date and I found out about the violin player he was seeing behind my back.

Sophomore year, Clarissa set me up with Vincent (Vincent, not Vince), a brooding cellist who practically her twin—his lustrous blond hair was even longer than hers. We went on a string of dates, and had sex a couple of times at my place. Things eventually fizzled out, though. I think he sensed I was hiding something from him, and it felt like he had secrets of his own. We split amicably, and I still saw him around the academy.

That was the sum total of my relationships, and it was pathetic. I hadn't been with a guy—in either sense of the word—in a year.

That, I told myself, was the only reason I dreamed of Darrell.

I didn't normally remember my dreams, and when I did, they were some abstract crap about flying—never about sex. This one, though, was all about sex. Full, Technicolor sex with sound effects and the feel of his skin under my palms. I remembered the touch of him against my thighs very clearly. In the dream, the skin there was flawless and smooth.

I woke in a tangle of sheets, feeling exhausted yet unsatisfied. This wasn't good—Darrell had already been filling my every waking thought, and now he was in my dreams, too?

I needed a second opinion. I needed to know if I should do something—pursue this, somehow—or be sensible and leave it well alone. I told Clarissa that I'd tell her all the gory details of the audition if we could go to Harper's for breakfast coffee and she agreed.

Harper's was one of two local places with a workforce almost entirely made up of Fenbrook students. The other place was Flicker, the bar I worked at. Harper's was a deli and a café, serving up half-decent coffee (depending who was brewing it), maple pecan twists that I pigged out on when I could afford them and huge sandwiches that formed the basis of most academy lunches.

We hooked up with Jasmine, too. Jasmine, an actress, had been part of our little group since freshman year. She had auburn hair down to her waist, huge pale green eyes and generous curves that stopped traffic when she wore anything low cut.

Clarissa bought us all coffee. Normally that made me uncomfortable—I made a big deal of making sure we always alternated, even though she had way more money than me. For once, though, I was happy to be pampered.

Clarissa brought over three steaming mugs. "So? Spill."

I went quiet.

"That bad?" Jasmine asked.

I stared at the little cracks in the tabletop and told them about the guy who burst in. I left out the part about him being hot, and the part where I'd danced imagining his hands all over me.

"*Idiot*," Jasmine said, as soon as I'd finished. "Probably just wanted to get a look at girls in Lycra."

"He probably has a *thing* for dancers," Clarissa told me. "I went out with one guy who wanted me to wear the whole thing: tights, leotard, shoes—*every* time we went to bed."

"Did you do it?" Jasmine was fascinated.

"Only for a couple of weeks. Then he wanted me to stand en pointe while he"—she exchanged a look with Jasmine—"Uh, *yeah*. So I got out."

Jasmine was doing her doe-eyed *I'm shocked but loving it* face. Seriously, that girl was going to be massive when she hit Hollywood. As usual, I sat there silently, not sure how to join in. Whenever the subject of sex came up, I sort of shut down. It wasn't that I didn't like sex, just that I couldn't imagine anyone wanting me.

Well...maybe one person.

"He asked me to dance for him," I mused. Then realized with a shock that I'd said it out loud.

"He *what?*" asked Clarissa, too loudly. Heads turned.

"Eww! Like, in his bedroom?" Jasmine wanted to know.

"Or maybe a lap dance. He probably wanted a lap dance," said Clarissa.

I bit my lip. I'd had the same thought when he suggested it. Well, maybe my mind hadn't gone straight to *lap dance*, but the idea had sounded weird. And yet...something about the way he'd said it had sounded so honest, so straightforward. I had a feeling that if a lap dance was what he'd wanted, he would have damn well asked for one and, worryingly, that thought didn't horrify me as much as it should have done. "He said he wanted a muse," I told them.

"A *muse?* Who is he, Van Gogh?" Clarissa asked.

"An engineer."

"What's his name?" Clarissa pulled out her laptop.

"Darrell," I said doubtfully. "Darrell Carner."

Clarissa's fingers skittered across the keyboard. She took a sip of her coffee as she waited for the results to come back and then froze, staring at the screen. I could see her eyes darting back and forth as she read. "*This* Darrell Carner?" she asked disbelievingly, and spun the laptop to face me.

It was him. He was in jeans and a shirt again, shaking hands with some guy in a suit, his floppy black hair soft and perfect. Something went through me when I looked at him, a crackling wash of energy that started in my face and soaked straight down, hitting the gas pedal on my heart and finishing in my groin. When I dragged my eyes away from the photo, I saw it was a news story.

Jasmine crowded in. "Ohmygod he's *hot!*"

Clarissa read the first line to us, one perfect eyebrow raised. "Darrell Carner today signed his third deal with Sabre Technologies, licensing his latest design for an estimated *twenty-six million dollars.*" She looked at me. "You left out that part."

"I didn't know." I was trying to fit *rich* together with the guy I'd talked to outside the audition, but the two refused to stick. "He didn't *seem*—"

"Did he offer to pay you?" asked Jasmine.

I had to think about it. "Well, yes, but—"

"Well then what the hell are you waiting for?" Jasmine was staring at me incredulously. "He's super-*gorgeous,* you should do it."

"Wait, wait..." I held my hand up. "A second ago he was a creep and probably wanted a lap dance. Now just because he's rich and"—I flushed—"and hot, he's suddenly okay? What if he's a rich, hot creep?"

"I don't think you can be rich, hot and a creep," Jasmine told me, then turned to Clarissa. "Can you?"

Clarissa shook her head happily. "No, if he's rich and hot then he's just kinky. *Adventurous.*" She saw my expression and sighed. "I'm *kidding!* Of course you should be careful. I'll drive you there and check you're okay. We'll do the phone call thing and everything."

Jasmine bounced up and down in her chair. "Ooh, ooh, we can have a duress code, in case he's got you tied up in a tutu."

I looked at both of them in turn. "I don't have a choice about this, do I?"

Clarissa shook her head. "This is easily the most interesting thing that's happened to you in about a year, and the thought of you possibly hooking up with some uber-bachelor...? No. You don't have a choice."

"Who says I even like him?"

Jasmine smirked. "We saw your face when you looked at his photo. Don't ever play poker."

Clarissa suddenly grinned as she remembered something. "Is *this* who you were—"

I kicked her under the table, my face turning red. I really didn't want to talk about the couch incident.

45

Jasmine leaned forward. "What? What did she do?"

Clarissa glanced at Jasmine, holding the secret over me like an axe. "Answer!"

I sighed and nodded and Clarissa squealed with delight. "You have to call him, right now. Before he finds some other dancer."

I hadn't considered that. Of course, he'd probably already found someone else. The idea made me suddenly angry—jealous, almost, which was crazy. "I can't. I don't have his number."

"He's famous," Clarissa told me. "We can find it."

"Facebook him," Jasmine suggested. She lived her life on Facebook, when she wasn't watching cop shows and *24* reruns.

I took out my phone, mostly because I was curious to see if there were other pictures of him on his Facebook profile. But something stopped me before I could enter his name in the search box.

I had a new friend request. From him.

***

I hit 'accept', because I didn't know what else to do (and I knew Clarissa would kill me if I didn't). My heart was thumping so hard everyone around me must have been able to hear it.

In less than ten seconds, I got a message from him.

"Hi."

I tried to come up with something witty, or clever, or flirty.

"Hi," I typed back at last.

There was a pause, as if he was choosing his words very carefully. Then, *"I'd really love to see you dance again."*

Why me? Why not any of the other dancers at the audition? Or...a horrible thought went through my head. Was he talking to all of us? For all I knew, he'd propositioned every one of them as they came out the door.

"You couldn't find anyone else?" I typed.

"I haven't asked anyone else."

Clarissa and Jasmine demanded an update. I was sitting pushed back from the table, so they couldn't see my phone's screen. "He hasn't got a muse yet," I told them. They both gasped and made *do it, do it* gestures.

Before I could type anything, though, another message arrived.

"Dance for me, Natasha."

I can't explain why, but seeing him use my name sent a thrill through me, rising and soaring in my chest. And there was something else, too. I remembered his voice, and now I imagined it saying my name. Growling it, almost. The thought of him doing that, of his hot whisper against my neck, sent a dark heat twisting down between my thighs.

"He just asked me," I told Clarissa and Jasmine.

"Check it's not a lap dance, before you do it," Clarissa said.

"Or check it *is* a lap dance, and do it anyway," Jasmine offered. Behind those big, innocent eyes lay a truly filthy mind.

"What would I have to do?" I typed.

"Just dance. Here at my house."

"What sort of dancing?"

"Ballet. Why, what did you have in mind?"

I flushed. "It's ballet," I told the others.

"Just checking," I typed.

"Check it's not nude," Clarissa told me.

I was taking a sip of coffee and spluttered it halfway across the table. "What?!"

"Just in case. He *is* paying you to dance at his house." She looked like she was half serious.

"You don't mean nude or anything, do you?" I typed back. And immediately regretted it.

"No. Why, would you like to dance nude?" It was impossible to judge his mood from the messages...so how come I just *knew* he was smirking?

"It's not nude," I told the other two tightly.

"Ask how much," Jasmine told me.

"How much?" I typed.

"How much would you like?" he replied.

Jasmine and Clarissa had moved around behind me now. I knew it was useless to try to stop them reading. They were right—this *was* the most exciting thing to happen to me all year.

"Say, like, $500 an hour," said Clarissa.

"I can't say that! That's nuts!"

"Opening bid," she told me.

"$500 per hour," I typed, hesitating before I finally hit the button to send.

Almost immediately: *"Fine. Is that a yes?"*

The world seemed to narrow down to a tunnel, everything but the screen of my phone fading out. I barely heard Clarissa and Jasmine gasp. And yet I didn't feel like things were sliding out of control, somehow. This complete stranger, with his crazy demand for a muse, felt *solid*. In fact, it felt like the only truly solid thing around me, besides the exercise bike and the sweet escape nestling inside the cigarette case.

What was this, really? On one level, it seemed legit—he didn't *seem* like some creep who really wanted a lap dance. But he was rich—*seriously* rich. Why had he pursued me, when he could have called any casting agency and found a dancer for a fraction of that price?

I remembered the way he'd looked at me, when he'd burst in. The way his eyes kept going to me, even when the others were dancing. Could he really be interested in *me?* My stomach lurched. Had I put on that good a show, convinced him that I was normal? Could I keep it up, and dance for him without him ever knowing the real me?

And was it just dancing he wanted, or was there the possibility of something more? The idea of getting close to someone, of risking them finding out the truth, should have terrified me. With him, the fear was being countered by raw desire at least as strong, and I didn't know which one was going to win.

I stared at the screen for a long moment. What was the alternative—carry on as I was? A year ago, I'd been cutting maybe once a week. Now I was up to once a day, and the exercise bike in the evenings. How long before that wasn't enough, and I broke down in class?

I had to take a chance.

I typed *"Yes,"* and then let out a long breath I didn't realize I'd been holding.

Almost immediately, he came back with *"Could you dance for me today?"*

What have I done? "Could you drive me—this afternoon?" I asked Clarissa without looking at her.

Her eyes were locked on the screen too. "I'll drive you anywhere you want. I have to meet this guy," she told me.

"3pm?" I typed back.

"See you then," he replied, and sent an address. Somehow, in the space of ten minutes, I'd become his muse.

Now what?

CHAPTER SEVEN

Natasha

CLARISSA SLOWED THE CAR until it was barely crawling along, then let it coast to a stop in a scrunch of gravel.

"This is *not* the place," she said disbelievingly.

I double-checked the address. It was.

We were thirty minutes out of the city and had turned off a quiet, tree-lined road onto a private driveway, iron gates swinging open in invitation. Now we were looking at—there was no other word to describe it— a mansion.

It was three stories high, built from huge stone blocks and looked like it'd been there a hundred years. A water feature stood in the center of the sweeping gravel driveway, a stone bowl big enough to swim in with white water spraying high into the air before arcing down to cascade over the sides. Parked in front of the house was a bright yellow sports bike with *Ducatti* stenciled on the side. Clarissa and I exchanged a look.

Darrell came out to meet us just as we were getting out of the car. He was wearing jeans and a t-shirt, the faded red fabric tight over his biceps. I watched his eyes take in me, then Clarissa. Then back to me. A little frisson of excitement went through me. I wasn't used to being the one a guy focused on.

"I'm Clarissa," she told him. "Natasha's friend." *And bodyguard who will knee you in the balls if you so much as touch her,* her smile seemed to say.

Darrell gave her a solemn nod and led us inside. I hadn't known exactly what to wear or what to bring, so I'd put on what I'd worn for the audition with my street clothes over the top, and pinned my hair up. I'd spent about five times longer on my make-up than usual, which hadn't gone unnoticed by Clarissa.

Inside it was even more intimidating, if that was possible. The hallway seemed bigger than our apartment, black and white tiles of shining marble stretching away into the distance. A chandelier the size of a small car hung overhead. Clarissa grabbed my arm and pulled me to her, so we could whisper to each other.

"*Do you believe this?*" she hissed.

"I know." I'd never been anywhere like it. At least Clarissa, with her rich folks and her trust fund, would feel at home. "We're in your world now," I told her.

Clarissa shook her head. "This is *not* my world. This is a long, long way from my world."

"Clarissa," Darrell asked, "Are you going to wait? It might be a few hours."

Hearing him say her name, I was suddenly jealous. I wanted to hear that deep, bass rumble wrap itself around "Natasha."

"Yes." Clarissa was keeping a very careful eye on him, as if he might pull out a ski mask and a hunting knife at any moment. "I'll wait."

"Great." He showed us into a breakfast kitchen. Everything was either spotless white tile or gleaming stainless steel. I wondered if he actually lived in the house, or just rented it out for photos.

On the tabletop were three catering pots of gourmet coffee and a basket—an actual wicker basket straight out of *Red Riding Hood*—crammed full of pastries. There were three different newspapers, a *Vogue*, a *Time* and a *People*.

"You knew she'd bring someone?" Clarissa asked.

"I thought she might," he told her. "We'll be downstairs."

"Downstairs?" My voice was almost a squeak. Three stories, and there was a downstairs, too?

"In my workshop."

I looked at Clarissa, but she gave me a nod. Whatever vibes she was getting from him, they were good ones. "I'll be right here," she told me.

She sat down, already reaching for the *Vogue*, and Darrell led me back through the hallway to a door at the back. It looked like a normal, white-painted wooden door, but when he opened it, we were looking into the bare steel walls of an elevator. He pressed the button at the very bottom: we were going three floors underground.

***

I wasn't ready for the sense of space.

I guess I'd prepared myself for some small, dark, claustrophobic room, maybe with a single light bulb hanging from the ceiling. I couldn't have been more wrong.

It was one huge, cavernous space. I realized that

the cellar must run the entire length of the mansion, maybe even beyond. The ceiling must have been a good fifteen feet high, but because the lights hung down from it, the ceiling itself just disappeared into blackness. The floor was smooth, flawless concrete.

The elevator had deposited us midway down the room's length. To my right was heavy engineering gear: huge machines whose function I could only guess at, big tanks of compressed gas and a crane's hook hanging down on a chain.

Right in front of me seemed to be where he did most of his work, and I could see immediately where his muscles had come from. There were workbenches littered with hunks of metal almost as big as me, and tools for pounding, cutting and welding it into shape. Farther on, there was a big, open space and then a sort of office area with a chair and desk and several large monitors. Was that where he'd sat and messaged me on Facebook? Directly over the desk, there was a poster for a local band I'd vaguely heard of called the Curious Weasels. I could see whiteboards full of math, too, and a coffee pot. I remembered the spotless kitchen upstairs. How much of his life did he spend down here?

This was no hobbyist's garage. This was a workplace, the modern equivalent of a blacksmith's forge. He must have spent millions building this place, constructing his perfect environment in which to build...what, exactly? I'd never heard of Sabre Technologies. Planes? Cars?

He didn't rush me, letting me take it all in. Then he led me over to the large open space.

"I figured...here. If that's okay." He looked around, as if checking there was enough space.

At the back of the room, I saw a big, wheeled cart some eight feet long. He'd draped whatever was on top—

his latest creation, presumably—in a white sheet, and then pushed it aside to make room for me.

I looked down at the bare concrete floor and traced the surface with the toe of my sneaker. "It's fine. Floor's going to be a little hard."

There was absolutely nothing sexual in that. Not until I glanced up. Suddenly I was looking straight into his eyes and something there made me catch my breath. It had been a perfectly innocent remark...so why was *I* the one flushing?

"For *dancing*," I explained. "Normally the floor's sprung, so that we get some bounce."

He looked at the concrete and nodded sagely, as if filing that away.

"It's fine, though," I told him. "It doesn't matter." And I started to unbutton my jeans.

He started, and sort of half-looked away.

"I've got dancing gear on underneath," I told him.

He nodded. Disappointed? I couldn't tell. There was a part of me that wished I *had* needed to get changed. Would he have turned his back? Would he have tried to sneak a peek?

Would I have wanted him to?

I felt that dark twist again, spiraling downwards between my thighs. For once, I didn't feel like things were slipping away from me. Here, in this crazy, rich man's world, three floors below a mansion, I actually felt grounded. I wasn't in the past or slipping towards it; for once, I was right there, in the moment. And it wasn't the place or even what I was doing that was making me feel that way...it was him. It was the way his attention was so completely focused on me, like I was the only thing in the world—I'd never been looked at so hard in my life. And underneath that cool, professional gaze, I could sense something else, something raw and sexual that made me heady and weak. Suddenly, the thin sweater and jeans I was wearing seemed insubstantial. What was it going to feel like in a leotard?

Time to find out.

I pulled off my sweater. Light from above cascaded down my body, making the black leotard shine. There was something weird about it—it wasn't like the harsh flicker of a fluorescent light. I looked up, squinting.

"It's called a light tube," he told me. "It's daylight, reflected down from the roof."

I unfastened my sneakers and kicked them off, and then I couldn't delay it any longer. My hands gripped the waistband of my jeans...and I stopped.

I told myself not to be stupid. I had tights on underneath, and I'd danced a million times before wearing the same outfit. I'd even danced in front of him.

But not like this, a little voice inside me said.

How could I dance just fine in front of a crowd, and yet just one person could reduce me to helpless mush?

I pushed down my jeans and stepped out of them. The tan tights where thin enough that I could feel the cool air of the cellar. I felt his eyes on my legs.

Of course he looked at your legs. He's a man. That doesn't mean—

"What would you like me to dance?" I asked, as much to silence my own thoughts as anything. I took my pointe shoes from my bag and then dumped it and my clothes out of the way.

"Your choice," he told me. "Nothing that'll be too uncomfortable on the floor." He stepped back and stood against the wall.

That threw me. Him choosing would almost have been easier, because now I had to pick between pieces I knew solid choreography for and could do really well and the ones I truly loved but wasn't as good at. I debated as I sat on the floor wrapping the ribbons around my ankles. In the end, I picked something in the middle. I loved it, I was pretty good at it, and there wasn't too much that would be problematic on the concrete floor.

He handed over his phone, set up like a remote for his music system, and I scrolled through until I found the piece I wanted. A few seconds later, the first bars filled the room, the notes drifting and echoing in the huge space.

I was moving, almost without thinking about it. This wasn't like the audition. There was no pressure to be the best and there were no inscrutable judges watching. I could almost have been on my own, dancing for pleasure.

I stepped, sank into the plié and glided into the turn, pushing harder than I normally would because of the concrete's friction. And then I made the mistake of looking at him.

And suddenly, it was different again.

It wasn't that he was looking at me with lust—at least, not on the surface. His eyes were as pure and clear as they'd been before, drinking in the movements and the flow. It was that he was watching me so intensely, relying on me to deliver...something. Inspiration? I couldn't imagine inspiring anyone.

It wasn't like a rehearsal, because I was alone. It wasn't like solo practice, because when I got a step not quite right or didn't nail a turn, I couldn't go back and try it again. I was performing. For him.

It wasn't the most challenging dance, especially that first section. So why was my heart racing? Why could one person make me nervous, when I'd danced for full theaters in our end-of-year shows?

I could feel his eyes on the shape of my extended leg as I leaned into a six o'clock arabesque, on the line of my arm as I straightened up. He wasn't just watching, he was *absorbing,* in some way I couldn't fathom, and whenever I messed up I felt like I was feeding him false information. *It shouldn't be like that! It should be like this!*

I felt like I was in a spotlight, in the very center of a massive stage and instead of an invisible audience I could forget about, I was being watched by the one guy I wanted—needed—to impress.

Yet something made it bearable, kept me teetering on the knife edge of tension without tipping over. When I made a mistake, he never did that little hiss of breath, never made me feel I'd got it wrong. He just watched, without judging and without commenting. I'd never seen someone so lost in the beauty of dance.

And gradually, I started to relax. My steps became more assured, my moves more graceful. When it came together, I actually felt lighter, the little glides of each bourrée almost effortless. I risked a few small jumps, careful on the concrete but wanting to give him something he'd remember. For the first time in my life, I was dancing not for an audience or for a judge or to play my part in a group, but *for* someone.

I was doing it to please *him*. A little flutter in my chest.

I was doing it to give him pleasure. A sudden, darker heat, lower down.

I realized I was only an arm's length from him. My last few steps had taken me forward, and normally I would have been near the front of the stage, staring out into the blackness. But here, in this underground room, it put me right up close to him. We locked eyes, and I was breathing harder than I should have been.

I sank down into a grand plié, and instead of just watching he crouched, his movements so harsh and cumbersome compared to my own, like watching a giant made of stone. He settled there, huge and hulking, and we stared at each another.

I rose, turned, feeling his eyes burning into my back. I pushed off into a pas de chat, airborne for just a second as both legs folded under me, then flowing into a turn as I landed. He was still watching me just as intensely, and he'd taken a step forward. I started to move towards him and something flickered down my body, like darkly sparkling starbursts that set every nerve humming. The dance called for me to take just a single step forward.

I took two.

I stopped no more than six inches from his body, close enough that he must have been able to feel the heat coming off me, my whole body glowing from the inside. My chest was heaving, my legs trembling. The leotard and tights felt like they were barely there, as if my body was throbbing nude before him.

The music stopped.

We stood there staring at each other. His eyes were just as clear and striking as before, but they'd lost that innocence, now. They were burning with something even more powerful: lust.

I thought I saw his shoulders twitch, as if his hands were moving, and I caught my breath, keeping my gaze fixed on his eyes. My lips parted just a little, my eyes closing. *He's going to kiss me! He's going to—*

He stepped back.

My eyes opened and I sort of swallowed and stepped back myself, turning away to hide my blush. For a few seconds neither of us said anything. I didn't know if he was looking at me and I didn't want to risk looking.

"Was that okay?" I asked, without turning.

"Beautiful." There was pain in his voice, as if he was sorry it was over. "Could you come back again...tomorrow?" he asked.

I nodded. "Sure." I retrieved my clothes and started pulling them on. It took me three tries to get my foot into the leg of my jeans. My hands were shaking as I picked up my bag.

When I turned, he was much closer than I expected. I almost walked right into the broad wall of his chest. We both froze, and I looked up at him again. His eyes brightly blue and—

And suddenly we were kissing. His palms were on my cheeks, thumbs brushing along the tightly-bound hair at my temples. His lips met mine and they were as gorgeously full and hard-soft as I'd imagined. They felt so *right,* so like the thing I'd been missing, that I let out a tiny shriek of astonished relief, and that opened my lips. His tongue was between them instantly, searching and pressing, a hot shudder travelling the length of me. I grabbed his arms to keep from falling.

As quickly as it started, it was over. He pulled back and we were both gasping. I felt like I was standing on a ledge no bigger than my feet, with plunging cliffs on every side.

He tried to say something, but no words came out. It was all too fast, too much. Being underground hadn't bothered me before, but suddenly the thought of all those floors above us, pressing down...

"I—I need some air," I told him.

He nodded, and led me to the lift. For three whole floors, we stood in silence, only a foot apart, neither of us daring to look at the other.

Just as the doors opened, he turned to speak to me. "Nat—"

The sound of a full-on screaming match hit us and we both snapped back to front.

CHAPTER EIGHT

Natasha

THE SHOUTING WAS COMING FROM the kitchen. Even before I was close enough to make out the words, I could recognize Clarissa's sharp, high voice. I'd heard her wield it like a scalpel to shred opponents—male and female—plenty of times. I was hearing it clash against the low rumble of a male voice, as solid and unyielding as a tank.

When I rounded the corner and saw him, I froze. Clearly, this was a home invasion.

The man was almost as big as Darrell, but with long, sandy-blond hair reaching down to his collar and a goatee. He was wearing a black t-shirt with faded, gothic writing on it—it could have been for a metal band or a biker gang, or some combination of both. His arms bulged under the deep tan of someone who lives their life outdoors, and his black jeans hugged his thickly-muscled legs all the way down to his biker boots. A complex tattoo covered one arm from wrist to sleeve.

I couldn't decide whether to run to Clarissa and pull her to safety or grab Darrell and push him towards the intruder, so I wound up staying where I was. My brain was still trying to catch up to this sudden shift in events—I hadn't even begun to process the kiss, yet!

Then what they were yelling began to sink in.

"Girl...you got a lot of nerve standin' there criticizin' my clothes when that skirt you're wearin' meant some woman in a sweatshop in China—"

"This is *Prada!* It's from *Milan!*"

"Some woman in a sweatshop in France has made a buck eighty-six for a day's work and a cow has died just so you can waggle your ass at the guys."

"Milan is in *Italy* and I don't *waggle* my ass and your boots are made of leather you—"

"My boots have been with me for ten years and they'll last another five. That's a good use of a cow. That cow died for a reason. Your skirt'll be in the trash next season 'cos it ain't *en vogue*." His voice was incredible. It was Californian drawl left over hot coals to bake and smolder.

"Excuse me for wanting to look good."

"Only place that skirt looks good is on the floor of some rich dude's apartment—"

Clarissa opened her mouth to speak and I rushed forward. "*What* is going on here?" I demanded. "Who is this?"

Darrell was rubbing the bridge of his nose. "Natasha, Clarissa: this is Neil. My oldest friend."

"We've met," Clarissa said darkly. She folded her arms and glared at Neil.

I looked between Neil and Darrell. "He's...You're his..."

"We were at MIT together," Darrell told me.

I looked back at Neil. "You were at MIT?" I flushed. "God, sorry! I didn't mean—You just—"

"Dress like a biker?" asked Clarissa.

"I am a biker," said Neil. "You got a problem with that, too?"

"What started all this?" From the way Darrell said it, this sort of thing wasn't unusual for Neil. Now I came to think about it, it wasn't all that unusual for Clarissa, either. But usually the men she met backed down.

Neil pointed at Clarissa, the muscles in his arm bulging under his t-shirt. "I walk in and she's readin' the *Times,* man, and she's all, like, *let's just execute anyone who doesn't drive a BMW."*

"I said a tax cut here and there for the people who keep the economy going—"

Neil took a step towards her, the buckles on his boots jangling. "Yeah, you just keep gouging it out of the bottom ninety percent with your silver spoon—"

"Enough! Neil, please don't argue with my guests. Clarissa..."

"*What?*"

Even Darrell blanched a little at the venom in her voice. "...nothing."

"Oh, so it's all on me?" Neil glared at Clarissa. "She can just sit up here and eat all the pastries—"

"I had *one! And they were for me!"* She took a step towards Neil, so that they were within touching distance. She had to look up at his face, now.

"They were for guests who were waiting. I'm a guest who was waiting!" He didn't move towards her. He just sort of *bristled,* and even I could feel the animal heat coming off him. I wondered what it was like for Clarissa, right up close.

"OK, OK, enough!" Darrell took a deep breath. "Neil, I'm sorry. I forgot you were coming over. Clarissa, I'm sorry I didn't get a chance to introduce you. Next time—"

"Oh, there won't be a next time," Clarissa told

him. "You think I'm going to sit here next time while some weed-smoking drop-out tells me how I should dress?"

"Hey, *one,* I only smoke for medicinal purposes, *two,* unlike Mr. Millionaire here I *got* my degree and *three,* as for how you should dress..."—he leaned forward and loomed over her—"I got some ideas on how you could dress. You want to hear them?" And he gave her a mocking, wolfish smile.

Clarissa gave a howl of rage, grabbed a pain au chocolat and stalked out. A moment later, we heard the front door slam.

In the silence that followed, I shifted my bag up on my shoulder. "I should probably...."

"Sure. Oh!" He pulled something from a pocket—a white envelope.

I took it, surprised, with no idea what it was. I caught Neil looking between the two of us, a suspicious look on his face, and hurried out before things got any weirder.

***

Clarissa gunned the engine and tore off down the driveway in a hail of gravel. The gates barely opened in time. "That guy!" she told me. "That guy!" And she gave a little scream of frustration.

"I won't ask you to go back there," I told her meekly. "Sorry."

She shook her head. "I wouldn't. Not for anything. God, he was so *annoying.*" She sighed. "How was your billionaire?"

"Millionaire."

"Same thing."

I had to think. "It was weird," I told her at last.

"Really? Dancing one-on-one for a slightly off multi-millionaire in his batcave?"

"It's not a batcave."

"What is it?"

"It's an underground...workshop."

"It's a batcave."

I started picking at a loose thread on the seat. Then stopped because this was Clarissa's BMW and she'd rage if she saw me. "Do you really think he's off?"

Clarissa shrugged. "If you had a mansion like that, would you spend all day down in the cellar?" She suddenly gasped. "Maybe he's a vampire!"

I poked her in the side. "I've seen him in daylight."

"Sunblock. Say what you want, next time I'm bringing garlic and a mirror."

"I thought you weren't coming next time?"

She didn't reply. I finally opened the mystery envelope and gave a gasp of my own. There were five crisp hundred dollar bills inside. I'd completely forgotten about the money part of the arrangement.

Clarissa watched me fingering the bills. "Level with me. Was it a lap dance?"

"Clarissa!"

"I promise I won't tell anyone, not even Jasmine." She considered. "Maybe Jasmine."

"*No!*"

"These days it's almost okay. I wouldn't see you any differently. I mean—"

"Okay, okay, *yes*. Yes, it was a lap dance and yes, we had sex. I went on top."

Clarissa's hands jerked on the wheel and we swerved, tires screeching. She fought for control while trying to look at me at the same time. By the time we recovered, I couldn't control the smile any longer and let it break across my lips. She pummeled me in the arm while letting fly with some choice curses.

I let the laughter bubble up from inside me. I couldn't remember when I'd last laughed—really laughed—and it felt good.

CHAPTER NINE

Darrell

THE LAST CHUNKS OF GRAVEL were still hitting the ground when Neil, chewing on a pastry, asked, "So, did you bang her?"

I closed my eyes and sighed. I loved the guy like a brother, but sometimes..."No. It's not like that."

"Uh-huh."

"She danced for me. I need inspiration."

"Uh-huh."

"That's all it was!"

"Was that an envelope of cash you gave her?"

"...yes."

Neil didn't even reply. Just looked at me and poured himself more coffee.

"It's not like that!"

"Like what?" He was watching me over the top of his coffee mug.

"It's not about the money."

"Oh. So it's love?"

I felt my face go hot. I wasn't ready to talk about that part of it with him. I barely understood what was going on myself. Jesus, was I blushing? What was I, a fourteen year-old girl? "No! It's business. I pay her to dance!"

"Uh-huh. Millionaire pays beautiful woman to dance for him in his cellar. That ain't suspicious at all." He drank about half his coffee without looking away from me. "You sure you know what you're doing?"

"I'm fine."

"How's the prototype? That fine?"

"Awesome."

"Liar. You figure out how to make it dodge yet?"

"No. Maybe. I don't know. That's what this thing with Natasha is about. I think there's something there, something to do with dancing."

Neil cocked his head to one side. "You going to put ballet shoes on a missile and have it pirouette out of the way?"

"Why do you have to be so literal? I don't know what the connection is yet. That's why I need to watch her dance some more."

"Uh-huh."

"Don't start that again." I poured myself some coffee. It was difficult to think, the kiss still burning in my mind. There was no way Neil could know what happened, right?

"You tell her about the missile? Does she know what she's helping you make?"

I said nothing.

Neil raised his eyebrows. "But you told her you make weapons for a living, right?"

"In a manner of speaking," I said shiftily.

"*What* manner of speaking?"

70

"The sort where I told her I'm an engineer."

Now Neil folded his arms and looked at me suspiciously. "You've never been secretive about it before."

He was right. I didn't hide what I did—I was proud of it. The world needed weapons, and *someone* was going to make them. I made the very best. So why hadn't I just told her, when I'd talked to her outside the audition? Or in our Facebook chat? Or downstairs, when she saw the workshop for the first time? Why had I flung a sheet over the missile, moments before she arrived? All of the girls I'd dated, the ones from the charity fundraisers and the horse races, had known what I did and they'd never had a problem with it. If they'd mentioned it at all, they'd claimed to be impressed. Why was she any different?

I shrugged. "She doesn't need to know."

"Mm-hmm." Neil picked up another pastry and started munching on it. "Because lying right from the first date always goes well."

"It wasn't a date!"

"There's an alternative." Neil paused for effect. "You could, you know, not make things that kill people."

My chest tightened. Neil and had come to an understanding about my work, after many years of drunken rants on both sides. He'd accepted what I did, but that didn't mean he liked it. "We can't all be flower children, Neil."

"The Bitch isn't going to be pleased."

"I wish you wouldn't call her that—it's childish. Her name's Carol."

"It's both accurate and appropriate. The woman is distilled bad karma."

I sighed. "How is it that you can have a problem with a respectable executive, but have no issue hanging out with someone called *Big Earl.*" The biker thing was more than dress-up and weekend rides for Neil. He was in pretty tight with one of the local motorcycle clubs, guys who'd leave you dead in a ditch without a second thought.

"Hey, those guys have honor and respect, man. They're like a brotherhood. And I mean it, Carol's going to be pissed."

"She'll get her missile." I topped up my coffee. "I'll get it working eventually."

"I wasn't talking about the missile."

It took me a second to figure out what he meant. "*Natasha?* Carol won't care about Natasha! It's none of her business! The company doesn't own me!"

"Uh-huh. You just keep telling yourself that, man. Hey, when are they coming again?"

" 'They'—Oh. *Clarissa.*"

Now Neil was the one looking shifty. "Yeah. I want to make sure I'm not here if she comes back."

I crossed my arms and watched him. "Uh-huh."

CHAPTER TEN

Natasha

THAT NIGHT, I TOOK A LONG LOOK at the bike and decided that—for once—I didn't need it. I just slid into bed and let my mind fill with thoughts of Darrell. Sleep took a while to come but I didn't mind. I had something solid to hang onto as I lay there in the darkness. Something to focus on.

Fantasize about.

....

Some minutes later, my hips strained upwards, my breath ragged as his mouth devoured my breasts, his hands roving over my ass. My fingers were his fingers, on me and in me...*God...*

I fell back against the pillow, sated. I lay there for a second, just relishing the feeling of being a normal girl, of being *happy*.

Then my fingers grazed the dressing on my thigh, the rough parallel lines of the scars beneath.

I wasn't normal. I wasn't normal at all.

I turned over, staring at the wall. The reality of what I did to myself, and why I did it, hit me like a freight train and I had to dig my nails into my palms to stop me sliding out of control. When it passed, though, it left something unexpected behind. A tiny, twisting thread of hope.

What if this was for real? What if, with him, I *could* be normal? When I was around him, I didn't seem to panic and slide down towards my memories so much. He anchored me, just as firmly as the punishment of cutting myself—maybe better. Maybe I'd wake up tomorrow and I wouldn't need the cigarette case.

Maybe.

***

The next morning, I figured I'd better stick to my routine, even if I wasn't going to cut. Too much change, too soon, couldn't be good, right?

My one deviation was to knock on Mr. Kresinski's door and pay him my rent—early. He was overjoyed at not having to chase me, and I figured it would buy me some slack if things went wrong in the future. I had no idea how long the arrangement with Darrell was going to last—or what it might turn into.

I got to the restroom while it was still empty, then sat there on the toilet seat for ten whole minutes debating whether to do it or not.

I didn't want to, but then I never *wanted* to. It wasn't a want; it was a need.

I thought of Darrell and felt like I'd be okay without it.

Then I thought about the corridors. The way everyone would push against me, between classes, not knowing who was in their midst. The long hours of practice, lined up with the other dancers—the *real* dancers, the ones who weren't fakes. The tension...dear

God, the tension of feeling that, at any moment, someone was going to announce what I'd done and everyone would discover the sort of person I really was.

I ripped down my jeans and swabbed at my thigh with an alcohol wipe. When I cut, my vision was blurry with tears and I went deeper than I meant to. Blood swelled and trickled and I swore and sobbed, blotting it with toilet paper. But even though I had to fix it, even though the line was ragged and torn next to all the neat ones, it still worked. I could feel the floor under my feet, feel my breathing returning to normal.

I slapped a dressing over it, looked down at myself and then cried again—big, hot tears. Because I knew that the thing I had with Darrell, whatever it was, would be gone in an instant if he ever found out.

***

By lunchtime I'd got things into some sort of shape in my head. OK, so I had a problem. But I was *functional*, right? I got by. As long as Darrell didn't find out, everything would be fine. Better than fine. Things could be great.

A little voice inside me told me I was kidding myself, but I crushed it.

The cafeteria at Fenbrook is your standard college eatery: trays of sodden mash potato, unidentifiable gray meat in sauce and wilted greens, long tables, cliques and noise. Only at Fenbrook you'd regularly see dancers in tights and tutus, grabbing a bite between rehearsals. Or a musician with his sax or guitar or violin next to him, watched as carefully as a favorite child. Or actors running lines while they ate, little snatches of Macbeth or Mamma Mia or CSI mixing together.

Clarissa and Jasmine were sitting across from me,

which made it feel a little like an interrogation.

"She still hasn't told me," Clarissa said to Jasmine, as if this was the cruelest torture possible.

"You still haven't *told* her?" Jasmine looked imploringly at me.

"Come on, Nat. You've had a day of mystery. What happened?" I could see Clarissa wasn't going to quit. Actually, now I'd had time to work through everything in my head, it'd be good to talk to them.

"He kissed me."

"*He kissed you* or *you kissed?*" Clarissa asked immediately.

That threw me. "Does it matter?"

They both looked at me as if I was crazy. *"YES!"*

I thought about it. "He kissed me. Definitely, he kissed me. But I kissed back. At least, I think I did."

"This was in the batcave?" Jasmine was almost bouncing up and down in her seat.

"It's not a—"

"So what happens now?" Clarissa interrupted. "Are you seeing him again this afternoon?"

"I'm dancing for him. I'm not—I mean, it's business, I think. It's not a date...is it?"

They both gave me that look again. Was I being incredibly naïve? Was this just some seduction technique he used—pay a girl to dance and then kiss her? But it didn't *feel* like that. The way he'd watched me...it had felt like he'd actually been studying me, not lusting after me. Most of the time.

"Can I come?" asked Jasmine. "I have to meet him!"

I started to nod. "Sure. Clarissa's not coming because...." I trailed off. Clarissa was shaking her head at me. "Clarissa *does* want to come," I said slowly, frowning. "Because...oh, wait. I get it."

Clarissa glared warningly at me.

Jasmine looked between the two of us, delighted. *"What?"*

I smirked. "Nothing."

***

As she slammed her door and checked her hair in the driver-side mirror, Clarissa told me, "You're wrong. I'm coming to watch out for you."

She'd put more lipstick on than usual, I noticed. "Mm-hmm."

"That guy's probably not even here."

She was in a DKNY dress, today. A *short* DKNY dress. I nodded at the Harley parked next to the Ducatti. "Mm-hmm."

Darrell opened the door just as I reached it. Glancing into the kitchen, I spotted Neil wearing, if it was possible, an even more faded and worn t-shirt and jeans than last time, as if he'd dressed as deliberately as Clarissa. There was a fresh basket of pastries and it looked bigger, this time.

Clarissa walked in behind me, saw Neil and huffed. "Oh, great."

Neil looked up and saw her. "Fantastic!" he shouted sarcastically. His acting wasn't any better than Clarissa's.

***

As soon as the elevator doors closed, things changed. I could feel it in the air...words unspoken and looks we didn't dare give each other. By the time we arrived at the workshop, I couldn't bear it any longer. We had to talk about what had happened, had to—

The doors opened and I just stopped and blinked. I stood there for so long that Darrell had to put his arm out to stop the doors closing again.

Where I'd danced before, where there'd been a big, open space, there was a stage.

Not some six foot, temporary platform for giving a speech. This filled the area from front to back and must have been fifty feet wide. Its top was three feet clear of the floor and its surface was smooth, polished wood.

I thought for a moment that it must have been a trick, that he'd stopped the elevator at a different floor or something. But this was definitely the room we'd been in the day before. And the smell of sawdust and wood polish hung in the air.

"How—" I began, "How could you *possibly* have...."

"Is it okay? You said a sprung floor was better."

I climbed up onto it and tried an experimental jump, then a proper grand jeté. There was just the right amount of give in the wood. It had been made by someone who knew what they were doing.

"It's great. But how...?"

He shrugged. "I called some people, straight after you left yesterday."

"They built this in an *evening?*"

"Oh, no. They worked through the night."

I blanched. The idea that someone would spend that much money, go to that much effort, for me...I took a staggering step backward.

He climbed up on the stage. "Natasha?"

I put out my hands. I only meant it as a gesture, to slow things down, but he took a step towards me at just that moment and suddenly my palms were against his chest. He had another of those faded t-shirts on and I could feel his warmth through the soft fabric. I drew in my breath.

If this was some seduction ploy, it didn't feel like it. Even when things went like *this,* when I could feel the blood rushing in my ears and hear my heart hammering in my chest. It didn't feel like it was coming from him *or* me. It felt like we were riding on a wave, swept along with it and barely managing to cling on.

"What is this?" I managed. "I mean...do you *really* want to see me dance? Or is this—"

"I built you a stage."

I stared into those beautifully clear eyes. I swore he wasn't hiding anything. "And is this really..." I sighed. "Is this really helping you? I mean...I can't see how I can inspire you to do..."—I cast my eyes at the workbenches, the computer screens, the shape under its sheet— "whatever it is that you do."

He stared at me for another second and then jumped down off the stage. Turning, he offered me his hand and when I felt how warm it was, when I saw my own slender hand captured in his, my stomach did a little flip-flop.

He led me over to the office area. There was a steaming mug of coffee on his desk and more in the pot. Sheets of paper covered in complex notation were scattered everywhere, and a small mountain of screwed up paper had buried what I assumed was a waste paper basket. He'd said the people he'd hired had worked through the night to build the stage. Had he been here all night, too?

He pointed to the whiteboards.

At first, I thought it was just scribbles, random lines with smudges underneath some of them. Then I looked more closely and the smudges resolved into equations. He'd written crazy small just to fit it all on— even with three whiteboards side by side. And then, finally, as I stared at it, as some of the detail dropped away and I began to see the shape of it, I thought I recognized it.

"Is that...?"

"It's you," he told me, and his voice was almost a whisper, as if he was scared that if he spoke too loudly, he'd destroy the fragile magic of it.

He'd captured—in some abstract form I could barely glimpse—the movements I'd made yesterday. The rotation of each pirouette, the arc through the air of each jeté.

I frowned. "But you didn't take notes." I looked around. "Is there a camera?"

He looked at the floor for a second, as if embarrassed. "I memorized it."

As he walked me back to the stage, I kept glancing at him, my mind whirling. This man, who Clarissa had declared a bit *off*, was a full-on genius in the purest sense of the word. I felt that little twist of hope inside me crushed. What on earth would someone like that see in me?

I remembered something, then. During the big argument between Neil and Clarissa, Neil had said Darrell hadn't graduated. Why not? With his mind, he could have aced any exam they'd thrown at him. It didn't seem like something I could ask him, though...at least, not yet.

I realized I had no idea what was going to happen, and maybe that's why I was almost lightheaded with anticipation.

I stepped onto the stage and looked down at him. It was strange, being taller than him for once, and I drank in every little detail. The thick, soft hair on the top of his head that I still hadn't run my fingers through. The way he managed to look so young, looking up at me with those big eyes, and yet so powerful, the muscles of his arms stretching the sleeves of his t-shirt.

I swallowed. I meant to say, *We should talk about the kiss,* but what came out was "What would you like me to dance?"

He hesitated, as if he, too, wanted to say something different. But what he said was, "Something with lots of aerial work, if you can."

This is crazy! We can't just ignore it! But I nodded and started to get changed. And immediately, it was different. Yesterday, I'd been unsure if he liked me. Today I knew he did, and he knew I knew.

I started to peel off my sweater...and stopped halfway, with it just beneath my breasts. I'd locked eyes with him, and my heart was suddenly thumping. *I have a leotard on, I have a leotard on.*

I pulled it the rest of the way off. His eyes didn't leave me once.

I kicked off my sneakers and unfastened my jeans. My legs emerged from the denim, soft whispers of nylon against the cloth. I saw him swallow.

I had to sit to put on my pointe shoes. As he stood there watching me, eyes eating up my every move, I was aware of how quiet it was. Just the two of us, in that huge underground room with no traffic noise, no birdsong, no nothing. Just the sound of our breathing and the creak of silk and leather as I wound and tied.

He passed me the phone again and I found the music I wanted. I should have been thinking about the steps—it was tougher choreography than last time—but I kept thinking about his lips, and the way his hands had felt on my face. Why didn't he want to talk about it? Had it all been a mistake, or did he just not know where to take this next?

The music started.

The dance began with a pas de chat, a quick little jump before I got to the big stuff. I flowed through the next few steps, then pushed off into the first of a series of grand jetés that took me most of the way across the stage—exactly the kind of aerial work he'd asked for. A pirouette and a piqué and I was moving directly towards him, relishing the glorious moment of weightlessness as I soared in another grand jeté, and another and another. On the final one, I landed only a foot clear of the edge of the stage. I'd have to be careful, when it came time to repeat that section.

A glissade took me back to the center of the stage and then a simple pirouette let me move into a fouetté, my leg whipping out to the side to power my turn. I heard a tiny intake of breath from him, as if I'd done something important. I turned again, again, trying to find a spot on the wall to focus on so I wouldn't get dizzy, but it was difficult in such an unfamiliar environment. The adrenaline was pumping now, the simple pleasure of dancing and the feel of his eyes on me combining to make me heady and careless. I came out of the final fouetté and launched into the first of three grand jetés that would take me towards him.

One, and I soared like a bird, one leg forward and one back, the rush of air delicious over my heated limbs.

Two, and something was wrong, but I couldn't see what it was. My feet were already preparing for the brief kiss of the stage, my muscles ready to push me back up for the final jump.

Three, and as soon as I took off I saw the danger, but it was too late to stop.

I was going to miss the stage. I was going to land not at stage level, but three feet further down. And instead of landing on springy wood, my legs were going to smash and shatter against cold concrete.

I let out a silent scream—

His hands caught me around the waist. My momentum swung me down, my feet sweeping an inch from the floor. He bent with me, then swung me back up and this time hooked an arm under my knees. And then I was in his arms, both of us panting.

The fear soaked through me—that aftershock of realizing how close you came. He held me as the chill passed. And then the feeling of his arms, strong under my knees and back, started to warm me again. I felt so...*safe*. Like he could hold me there forever, if I needed it.

I looked up into his eyes.

His lips came down on mine. A gossamer touch at first, then firm and hungry, my own mouth responding just as needfully. He sank down, until he was kneeling on the floor with me draped across his knees. I reached up and grabbed his shoulder, pulling him down further so that we were lying on the floor, him on top. The concrete should have been freezing through my leotard. It wasn't. It felt like we were warming the whole area around us.

His hand was on my hip and I gasped not so much from the touch as the idea that he was touching me. He slid it up my side, tracing my waist through the smooth black Lycra. Up to my chest, to the side of my breast. My whole body tensed, wanting him to, but he held back. He smoothed over my bare shoulder and I writhed under him and then we were kissing again, both of us breathing in slow, shuddering gasps. Like before, it felt like we weren't in control. It felt like this was just happening and all we could do was watch.

He broke the kiss, my lips throbbing and damp. His hand was on my stomach, now, his warmth spreading through the tight material and waking a dark, animal craving inside me. He started to slide it higher, the whole time keeping his eyes on mine, checking it was okay.

I stared straight back at him.

Up, over my core. Up, his fingertips tracing along my ribs. The very edge of his hand brushed the underside of my breast and I parted my lips a little wider, but I didn't tell him to stop. And then he was right on it, his palm smoothing over the softness of it, and I wanted to grind my hips and arch into him because it felt so goddamn good.

He squeezed, so, so gently, and I caught my breath, hot spirals radiating outwards through my body.

"Clarissa is upstairs," I panted.

He stared down at me and then nodded and released my breast. His hand found mine and he stood, pulling me up with him.

"What is this?" I asked him again, and this time my eyes told him I wasn't going to let him escape without a proper answer.

"I don't know. I...I really like you. A lot."

The way he said it—so clumsy, so *him*—made me swell up inside. That tiny glow of hope was shining brightly now, pushing back the fear.

But it was crazy. "You don't even know me," I told him, my voice scarcely more than a whisper. "And I don't know you."

He looked at me for a long moment, and then nodded, and sat down on the edge of the stage. I sat down next to him.

He looked at me steadily. "Ask me anything."

Weird how, when you're suddenly put on the spot with a person you're insanely curious about, all the questions go out of your head.

I looked around the room for inspiration, then up at the mansion, above us. "Are your parents rich?"

"My parents are dead. No, they weren't rich. It's my money."

There was something strange about his answer. He wasn't being defensive, or bragging about the money being his. It was more like he was owning up to it.

I went to ask him something else, and then stopped. "Ask *me* something. Otherwise it feels like I'm interrogating you."

"When you danced in that audition...what were you thinking about?"

Did he know? "You," I said simply. "I felt like I was dancing with you." I wasn't used to telling the truth. It felt odd.

"And before that, when you were angry. Was that me?"

God, he'd noticed that, too? Even then, he'd been observing me, able to see the difference between the emotion in the dance and what I was actually feeling. "Yes," I said, for safety.

"Really?" He looked hurt.

"No." But I said it in a way that said *don't ask,* and he didn't. "How did they die?"

He blinked a couple of times and I thought he wasn't going to answer. Then he turned away for a second.

"Wait," I told him. "It doesn't matter. Sorry."

He drew in a deep breath. "Car bomb." Each word dragged like a rusty blade from his chest.

I swayed back on the edge of the stage and pulled my legs up. Twisted on my ass and slid myself towards him, then sat down behind him, so he was between my thighs. I wrapped my arms around his neck, my head pressed up against his. "Sorry."

"Are yours alive?"

I felt myself shake my head. "No. Foster parents,

since I was fifteen." I could hear the pain in my voice, and I knew he heard it too.

We lapsed into silence.

"Do you want—I mean, I wasn't sure if you—" He stopped and started again. "Do you want to keep doing this? Dancing for me?"

"Yes! God, yes, I love it. But...not if it's just...." I shrugged my shoulders, hoping he could feel it against his back. "I mean...you don't have to pay me to be here."

He craned around to look at me. "Does the money make you uncomfortable?"

"Not as long as it's for the dancing."

"It's for the dancing."

"And you really need it? It really helps, to see me dance?"

He nodded, and jerked his head towards the whiteboards. "I really need it."

I took a deep breath. "Then I want to keep doing it. But I'd like to—Can we do something else? Together? A date?"

He smiled. He didn't smile often, but when he did it was light-up-the-room fantastic. "I'd like that."

***

We hesitated as we left the elevator, listening for the shouting. There wasn't any. Had one of them left? Were they sitting reading the newspapers?

Then, as we got closer, there was the crash of something breakable hitting the floor. I turned to look at Darrell. "Oh." I was just a little disappointed. I thought I'd sensed something between them. I thought that was why Clarissa had worn *that* dress.

We rounded the corner. "*Oh!*" I said again, very quietly.

Clarissa was half-lying on the table, the newsprint from the *New York Times* rubbing off onto her dress. Her outstretched arm was what had just knocked a mug off the table to shatter on the floor. One of the catering pots of coffee was lying on its side, hot coffee glugging out across the table—luckily, away from her.

Neil was between her legs, one hand hiking her already short dress up almost to her hips, the other under her back. It was almost violent—I would have been worried, had Clarissa not been kissing him with wild, unrestrained hunger.

For a second I worried about disturbing them. Then I realized they were completely oblivious to us. I exchanged looks with Darrell and got another of those fantastic smiles.

We waited by the front door. "Tomorrow night?" he asked me.

"I have to work. Monday?"

"Monday. I'll call you."

We both glanced towards the kitchen again, as if afraid of being caught—why?—and then he was kissing me again, soft and gentle, a teasing kiss that sent heat rippling down my back. I had to stop myself giggling. How long had it been, since I giggled?

I closed the door behind me, making sure to give it a good slam that Clarissa and Neil would hear. Sure enough, she came out a few minutes later.

"*That man!*" She was almost spitting out the words. "Smart enough to know better, but he's all— *urgh!*"

"Mm-hmm." Her hair was mussed, as if from strong hands stroking through it. We climbed into the car.

"Remind me never to come here again with you. I can't stand to be in the same room with him."

"Mmm." I thought about telling her that her lipstick was smeared, but decided it was more fun not to.

CHAPTER ELEVEN

Natasha

SATURDAY NIGHT AT FLICKER. There's an unwritten rule that, if you have to work a weekend shift, your friends come along as customers to keep you company. Clarissa had to rehearse, but Jasmine was there and she'd brought Karen.

Flicker was a bar, opened twenty years ago by some group of low-budget filmmakers who needed somewhere to meet—and a way to make money when their films kept bombing. They'd kept the lights low—like, trip-over-something low—and invested in hundreds of screens, hung all over the place like an art gallery. The screens showed random, classic scenes from movies, minus the sound, which made for a pretty good conversation filler if you were on a date that wasn't going well, or could lead to full-on group movie karaoke if you were with friends and a movie from your teen years came on.

Jasmine and Karen were sitting at one of the small, black tables. I could tell they'd argued over where to sit and reached a compromise. Jasmine would have wanted to sit in the very middle of the bar, while Karen would have pleaded for a corner. They'd wound up against the wall, but midway along it so there was plenty of passing man-traffic for Jasmine to look at.

Karen was a musician. In fact, she was the most musiciany musician I knew. Let me try to explain.

Fenbrook was divided into three camps: dancers, actors and musicians. Now of course we all got along just fine and had plenty of friends in all three disciplines, but there were still stereotypes and prejudices. They were gently mocking rather than cruel, but they were still there.

Every discipline thought it worked the hardest. We dancers pointed to our aching legs and sore feet, and the fact we were physically fitter than anyone else. The actors liked to say that their emotional toil was the worst ("I had to *live* being a drug addict for a week—do you know what that's *like?*"). Musicians moaned about the endless practice they had to do.

If Fenbrook was a high school, then actors were the cool kids everyone was jealous of (seriously, how many famous dancers do you know?), we dancers were the jocks and the musicians were the geeks. Like I said, it was a gentle, loving stereotype. We all worked our asses off and we knew it. But musicians did have a reputation for being the quiet, studious ones and Karen was the living embodiment of that.

She was a cellist—I swear, her cello case was bigger than she was—and generally regarded as the best musician Fenbrook had. Possibly the best student the academy had, *period*. She was a bit of a control freak, practicing before anyone else arrived and staying long after everyone else had finished. She was also seriously posh. Her family might not have had as much money as Clarissa's, but her accent was pure upper class Boston.

Jasmine and I had taken care of her since we all met as freshman. She was friendly enough, if a little intimidating, but I sometimes wondered if she understood the concept of *having fun*. It felt like she begrudged every moment she spent away from her music, until we almost felt guilty asking her to come out with us. She'd remained single, despite our best attempts to set her up with guys. Even as I walked up to their table, I could see Jasmine eyeing up guys for her.

"What about that one? No, not *him—eww!—him!*" I turned and followed her eye line. There was an actor there I vaguely knew—Billy something. Good smile, good body...and he knew it.

Karen shook her head quickly and looked up at me, hoping for rescue.

"Leave the poor girl alone," I told Jasmine. "She's happy single."

"No one's happy single. The happy singleton is a myth put about by a conspiracy of happy couples, to make unhappy single people feel even worse. We should be *proud* of our unhappiness." Jasmine thumped the table with her fist. "Now fill us in. What's the latest from the batcave?"

I bit my lip. There was so much to tell...falling off the stage, the kissing, the—I flushed. Not to mention that we were going on an actual, proper date on Monday. I'd told Clarissa, who'd hugged me and told me to be careful, still blissfully unaware that I'd seen her and Neil kissing. But I'd told her in the car, right after it happened, and now that I'd had time to think, it was harder. Things with Darrell felt too magical, too fragile...like a soap bubble. On the other hand, I couldn't *not* tell them....

"Do you want another one of those?" I asked, trying to change the subject. Each of them had just finished a Pretty Woman—all the cocktails in Flicker were named after movies. Pretty Woman was actually one of the lighter ones; you didn't order a Dark Knight or a Hunger Games unless you didn't have anything to do the next day.

Karen shrugged, as if she'd rather be working her way through some Brahms. I wasn't going to get any help there.

"You think you're getting out of it that easily?" Jasmine asked me. She looked at her empty glass, edible glitter and pink goo coating the inside. "Okay, then. Go! Go to the bar, but on your return you will relay every morsel of said story, that we may swoon over you and your prince!" I could always tell when she'd been rehearsing Shakespeare.

I wished I was more like her—loud and funny and flirty. I might not have been a Karen, but I still spent a lot of time brooding. Not to mention what I did to myself when I was on my own.

A warm glow spread through me as I remembered the kiss. All I had to do was make sure he didn't find out who I really was, and I could be as happy as Jasmine. I thought back to what he'd said about his parents. I'd better steer clear of that subject, or inevitably it would lead us onto my own past.

As I waited for the barman to make two more Pretty Women, I gazed around the bar. I always felt I could relax in Flicker, that all of us were off duty here. There were some bars in New York where the actors went with the specific intention of being discovered. Here, almost everyone was either from Fenbrook or hung around with that crowd. We weren't trying to impress anyone here, except maybe each other.

Not that we didn't get groups of non-Fenbrook guys—outsiders—coming into Flicker. Come on, the place had a reputation for having actors and dancers working there, of course we did. But groups of actors and dancers can be cliquey and protective, and the guys usually left disappointed. Plenty of times I'd heard Jasmine or Clarissa issue a withering put down to some guy who'd got a little too gropey, or come out with some lame line. Don't ever, ever, ask a dancer if she can put her ankles behind her ears.

I caught myself wondering if that was why I liked Darrell so much—because he hadn't approached me in a dark bar, looking to sleep with me. He'd wanted me as a dancer first, and everything else second. It made me feel like I was worth something, like I had something to offer. I really believed that, if I'd rejected his advances, he still would have wanted me to dance for him. Not that I had any intention of rejecting his advances. I smiled a secret smile, the memory of his hands on me sending a swirl of excitement down between my legs. I coughed, self-conscious, and looked around the bar again to stop myself completely zoning out.

I couldn't stop thinking about him, though. About those whiteboards, and his interpretation of my dancing, the moment when I'd caught a glimpse of his amazing mind. I'd been a little intimidated at first, but once he'd told me and—I flushed—shown me that he was really interested in me, I was just in awe. I realized that I was as fascinated by his ability to create as he was by my dancing.

I took another look around. It was a fairly quiet night. After two years at Fenbrook and nearly as long working at Flicker, I knew all the regular faces and I didn't see anyone Karen or Jasmine would want to flirt with. I silently cursed. Part of me wanted there to be a distraction, because without one I was going to have to tell them all about Darrell.

I brought over their drinks, together with a water for me and took the money. And then I was out of time. They stared at me hungrily, even the aloof Karen clearly desperate to know.

"Okay, okay." I took a deep breath. "I was dancing for him—"

"Naked?" asked Jasmine.

"What? No, not naked! Where did you get 'naked' from?"

"I was just checking. I thought I might catch you out. So it's really not a sex thing?"

"No! He's getting inspiration from me."

They both looked at me doubtfully.

"What is he, again?" asked Karen. "A choreographer?"

"No..."

Karen frowned. "An artist? Is he painting you?"

"No. He's an engineer."

They both looked at each other. I sighed. "It all makes sense when you see the whiteboards. It's about how I move in the air, and...." I trailed off. "Things."

"So...what is he actually building? A dancing robot?" Jasmine's expression wasn't cruel—she was genuinely trying to understand. But I didn't have a good explanation to give her.

"I don't know." I spread my arms wide. "But what does it matter? He's inspired by me."

Jasmine looked as if she didn't completely buy it, but she nodded. "Okay, so you were dancing for him..."

"And I fell off the stage. And he caught me. And then he kissed me."

Both of them did a delighted little gasp. Karen actually put her hand to her heart. "That is *so* cute!"

Jasmine told me.

I beamed, the pride swelling up inside me. Jasmine clinked glasses with me.

"Do you think he guessed?" she asked.

"Guessed what?"

"Guessed it was deliberate."

My jaw dropped open. "It wasn't deliberate!"

They exchanged glances. Then Jasmine asked, "You fell off the stage?"

"Yes!"

"Do you do that a lot?"

"No, but...it was a new stage! He'd only just had it built—"

"He *built* you a stage?" asked Karen, eyes wide.

"I know. I wasn't used to the size of it, and I was...distracted. I was thinking about him, and I went off the edge."

"So you *actually* fell and he caught you?" Jasmine blinked, astonished. "That's...genuinely romantic. And klutzy of you." She punched me on the arm. "Idiot. You're lucky you didn't break something. Tell us about the kiss."

"He caught me and held me in his arms and kissed me," I said, all in a rush. "And then he sort of knelt,"—I leaned forward—"and we were down on the floor, him on top of me...." They both leaned in, so we were in a huddle. "And then...God, he had his hand on me—"

"*Where?*" asked Karen, with surprising urgency.

"My breast—"

"Wait," said Jasmine. "Is there sex? Because if there's sex, I want popcorn."

"No, no sex." I realized I was grinning. Actually grinning. Finding someone I connected with seemed so miraculous, and the whole thing felt so new and exciting, that I'd been scared that even talking about it would somehow end the spell and destroy the whole thing. Now that it was out in the open, that seemed ridiculous. I was glad I'd told them. "And that's it. We're going on a date on Monday."

"Is he paying you?" asked Jasmine.

"No!"

"Okay, so an actual date. Wow. Where?"

"No idea. He's going to call me." And spontaneously, we did a ridiculously girly little *squee* of shared excitement. The coming week was going to be great.

CHAPTER TWELVE

Darrell

I WAS ON MY BACK, lying on a wheeled sleeper with the missile suspended a foot above me. I'd stripped down to a vest and an old pair of jeans while I drained the fuel and hydraulics, knowing I'd get covered in it. Sure enough, my hands were already blackly sticky with oil and from there it was transferring to my clothes. It didn't help that I was using the front of my vest as a rag every time my hands got too slippery. I was probably going to have to bin everything I was wearing when I was done.

It was Sunday, and I wanted to get as much done on the missile as I could, knowing I'd be taking Monday night off for my date with Natasha. Just the thought of it made me smile. I normally begrudged taking even a few minutes off to eat, but for her I'd have happily disappeared for a month.

A buzzer sounded, telling me a car was at the gates. I cursed. If it was another salesman, I was going to go berserk.

I slid out from under the missile and checked the gate camera. A convertible Aston Martin in racing green. *Great. Just what I need.* The gates were already opening—she had her own remote for them, and her own key for the house.

It was only a few minutes before the elevator doors opened and I heard the harsh click-clack of her designer heels on the concrete. I was already back underneath the missile, which was probably rude. I didn't care.

"I see." Her cut-glass British accent echoed around the huge space. "I travel thousands of miles to see you, and you don't even greet me?"

I kept working. "It's only four hundred miles to Virginia. You didn't come to see me, you came to check on the project, and shop. And I'm greeting you now. *Hi.*"

I heard her shift papers around on my desk so that she could perch on the edge and knew, *knew* that she'd be taking a careful look at my screens at the same time. "Darrell! What a thing to say! Seeing *you* is always my top priority. The project's completely unimportant."

I put my hands on the missile's casing and gave myself a push. The sleeper, with me on it, rolled out and I came to a halt only a few feet from where she was sitting.

Carol was wearing a very tight, very short gray skirt—, which I suspected was for my benefit—and a black turtleneck sweater. Her long dark hair lay in gleaming waves down her back. When we'd done our first deal, I'd hacked the Sabre Technologies personnel files to see who I was dealing with, and that was the only reason I knew she was now 38. She could have passed for five years younger—maybe more.

"Are you looking up my skirt?" she asked, raising one eyebrow.

I ignored that and stood up. The relationship we had was...complex. When I'd first met her, she'd been an up-and-coming research and development exec, eager to make her name, and I'd been a college kid with a killer design but no idea what to do with it. My success had fuelled her success, and although she was now head of R&D with about a hundred contractors to oversee, she was still focused on me, and how much money my next weapon was going to make her company.

Nothing had ever happened, but in those first few months when I'd been going through hell, we'd got closer than we probably should. I probably could have made more money working with another company—Sabre was tiny compared to some of the better-known names in the industry—but the money wasn't what drove me.

I looked at the missile and she followed my gaze, then slid from the desk and came to stand behind me. She didn't actually touch me, but she was close enough that I could smell her perfume.

"Tell me. What will it do?"

She knew I couldn't resist talking about my work. With Carol, I knew there wouldn't be any shock or outrage. She understood why I did it—she *wanted* me to make the most efficient killing machines possible.

Sabre Technologies didn't employ me, but they fed me projects—problems to solve. I didn't accept any money from them in advance and they didn't have to buy what I created. That was the way I wanted it: I put enough pressure on myself without having to work to a deadline. Of course, me being out of their control made them edgy—hence the monthly visits from Carol.

I walked around the missile. "When I finish the new system, it'll be able to dodge incoming interceptors. Maybe go from a thirty or forty percent chance of reaching its target to an eighty or ninety percent chance."

Carol beamed at me. "Fewer missiles to do the same work."

I smiled coldly. "Or same number of missiles, but more cities destroyed." I stopped abruptly. I'd meant it as a light-hearted comment, but I could feel my stomach clenching. That thought wouldn't have bothered me a week ago. Why did it now?

Carol cocked her head at my tone and looked questioningly at me, but I just brazened it out. Eventually she relented and looked towards the stage. "And what is *that?*"

"That's for Natasha."

She did a good job of looking thrilled for me. If I hadn't known her so well, I would have bought it.

"*Natasha?* Have you been taking time away from the project, you *bad* boy?"

"No, actually. She's a dancer. She's been—" I knew she wouldn't understand. "She inspires me."

"Oh!" Carol clapped her hands together. "A dancer! I see. Your own private club, right where you work. Doesn't she need a pole, though?"

"She's a ballet dancer." I could feel my jaw clenching. She knew exactly how to press my buttons.

"Oh I *see!* She's your *muse!* How very Da Vinci. Are you fucking her?"

I'd gone back to working on the missile while we talked, and I dropped the spanner I was holding. "*What?* That's—That's none of your damn business!"

"Oh. So *yes,* then. Do be careful, Darrell. The last thing I need is to be asking our lawyers to help you fight a paternity suit—"

I'd picked up the spanner again, but now I hurled it across the room and heard it clang off the stage. "Goddamnit, Carol you're not my mother!"

She blinked at me. "Oh, my word. Are you in *love*

with her?" She somehow managed to sound hurt, amused and patronizing all at the same time.

I could feel myself bristling. I glared and said nothing.

"I must meet her! Tell me, what's the attraction?" She leaned closer and whispered theatrically. "Can she put her ankles behind her ears?"

I took a threatening step towards her, but she just smiled sweetly. I knew I could never scare her: she knew the hold she had over me. I took a deep breath. "The missile will be ready in two weeks, maybe three. Until then..." I looked pointedly at the elevator.

She stood so that the missile was between us and stroked it almost lovingly. "I *love* to leave you in peace. But unfortunately...."

My heart sank. "What?"

She bit her lip as if she dreaded telling me. I could tell she was cackling inside. "You're wanted in Virginia."

"*What?* I can't. Carol, I really can't. I have to work on this."

"Take some extra time over it. We understand. You'll only be away a week."

"A *week?*"

"R&D show and tell. All the company bigwigs. Mucho important, darling, or I wouldn't ask."

I shook my head. "Tell them no. Sorry, but no."

She gave an elaborate grimace. "Oh dear. And I already told them you'd come."

I went to hurl something across the room, but I'd already used the spanner. "Why?!"

She pouted. "I *did* drive all the way from Virginia to pick you up. We can leave tomorrow morning."

I groaned. My date with Natasha was the next evening. I'd have to call her and delay it– for a whole week. "Is there any way at all I can get out of this?"

She grinned and shook her head. "It'll be *fun*. You and me, in the Aston, blasting down the highway...." She gave me her sad puppy eyes. "You wouldn't...you wouldn't want me to get into trouble, would you, Darrell?"

I sighed. I hated her, but my whole career was tied to her. "Fine. Now please can I work?"

"Well! I know where I'm not wanted! Do keep me updated, Darrell. I worry about you." She came over and, before I could stop her, she was kissing me on the cheek, her lips cold and rubbery. I brushed my fingers along her hips and she gave a little gasp of delight, eyes shining, before she walked off to the elevator deliberately swinging her hips.

I allowed myself a tiny smirk, watching not her ass but the twin sets of black, oily marks I'd just left on her skirt. And then I tried to figure out how I was going to tell Natasha.

CHAPTER THIRTEEN

Natasha

IT WAS ONE OF THOSE LAZY SUMMER days when time seems to run like treacle. Clarissa and I were sprawled on a bench with the sound of Vivaldi wafting over us and as the sun baked my upturned face, I replayed my kisses with Darrell. Had the first one been better, or the second one, after I'd fallen off the stage? I smiled contentedly and decided I needed to rerun them a few more times to be sure.

We were in Central Park, sitting with Karen and the rest of her string quartet as they played for passers-by. It was a weekly event for them, a charity thing. I secretly suspected that the only reason Karen did it was because it let her play while satisfying her friends that she was doing something semi-social.

The sun and the music meant there was no need to chatter—we could both just sit there with our thoughts, and that was exactly what I needed. I—reluctantly—moved on from the memory of the kisses.

He'd said he liked me—a lot—and I sure as hell liked him. More than that, maybe. It felt a lot like I was starting to fall for him. Funny how we say that, but it feels like the exact opposite, like I was being filled with helium and rising up like a balloon every time I thought of him. I was excited, too, filled with a kind of giddy energy whenever I thought of our date the next day. *I'm drunk on him,* I thought, and grinned.

But it was too early to be feeling like that. Wasn't it?

I'd never known anyone quite like him. His drive was staggering—okay, so there were some signs that maybe he spent a little *too* much time down in that workshop, but I was in awe of his ability to just focus on something so determinedly until it was done. The guys I'd dated in the past looked aimless by comparison.

The quartet finished the Vivaldi to a smattering of polite applause and immediately moved onto Mozart's *Eine Kleine Nachtmusik.* I always liked that piece, and this close to the instruments it had the same effect as cranking your music up on your headphones: life felt like a movie. When the flamboyant final movement began, combined with my mood, it made me want to—

"We should dance," I said suddenly.

"We already do. Where have you been for, like, a decade and a half?"

"No: right now. We should dance."

Clarissa turned and stared at me. "*Here?* You want to dance here, in front of...."—she looked at the passers-by—"the masses?"

I nodded. I was grinning. I couldn't stop grinning.

"You get nervous even when it's people you know—" she started.

"I'm doing it," I told her, and got up.

"You're in *sneakers!*"

I ignored her. I couldn't help myself, and I mean that seriously. The sun and the music and being there with my friend all conspired to make the day feel magical. Ballet dancing in the middle of Central Park just felt like the sort of thing I should do. And I knew the catalyst for all of it was underground, toiling away even on a weekend, biceps bulging as he lifted one of those big hunks of metal, blue eyes focused on some detail of his work. I thought of the way it felt when they focused on me, and went weak inside.

And then I was moving as if in a dream. Two light steps onto the path and then a turn, awkward in my sneakers, but doable. I had loose, soft combat trousers on because I hadn't wanted my legs to fry, and a Fenbrook t-shirt—almost street dancing gear.

I didn't really think about what I was doing, letting the music carry me. Arms up, turn, into a pas de chat. Dancing in sneakers was like trying to drive a car in rain boots, but it didn't stop it being fun. I turned and leaned into a penchée, one leg up in the air, and was vaguely aware of people watching, moving outwards to give me space. I moved back towards the bench and suddenly Clarissa was there next to me, gliding past me as we swapped sides. We exchanged smiles as we passed and she gave me a little shake of the head, as if to say *what have you gotten me into?*

I jumped up onto the bench and went into first arabesque and then into a promenade, pivoting in little movements like a ballerina in a music box. Clarissa was doing the same thing and for a second we were perfectly in sync. There was applause as the piece came to an end. We stood there grinning at each other, holding the position as a few people took photos. When we finally jumped down, Clarissa came straight over to me. "You and your billionaire—you've—"

"Don't say it!" I said quickly.

"You're in—"

"Don't! I'm not. I don't think I am. Maybe I am." I could feel myself blushing. "I really like him."

Karen came over. "You should do that more often," she told us, holding up the top hat they used for collecting the money. "We doubled the take on that one piece."

We were debating where to go for coffee when my phone rang.

***

I hung up and stared at the ground. It was no big deal, I told myself. He was going to call me from Virginia. We'd have our date the next week, when he got back. He hadn't sounded like he was doing it lightly—he'd sounded genuinely sorry, in fact.

I wasn't panicking, didn't feel like I was sliding out of control, but I was frustrated. *Just when things were going so well!*

I was suddenly angry with myself. I was letting myself get in far too deep, too fast. He probably didn't even feel the same way. I mean, he'd said he liked me, but that wasn't the same as how I felt—or *maybe* felt. Some time apart would stop things moving too fast. It was probably a good thing.

So why did the week ahead seem to stretch out in front of me like a marathon?

CHAPTER FOURTEEN

Darrell

THE ASTON MARTIN WAS TECHNICALLY MINE–a gift from Sabre when they'd landed a big deal based on my first design. But Carol had coveted the car from the very start and, since I was more of a bike guy, I'd let her drive it whenever she visited. Within weeks, she'd started doing those puppy-dog eyes at me and the car moved to her garage in Virginia. I hadn't minded too much–it had suited her, being British, and I'd been a kid, starry-eyed at landing his first deal–I figured I owed her. Four years later, I knew she thought of it as hers. I'd really have to get round to formally signing it over to her, at some stage.

Carol threw the car into the next bend, letting the back slide out just a little and then powering out of it with a squeal of tires. It didn't distract her from the rant she'd been on since we left New York.

"There wasn't even any point trying to wash it. I had to bin it, and I'd bought that skirt *two weeks ago.*"

I shrugged. "It was an accident." We both knew I was lying. But it was no more than she'd deserved, for the way she'd talked about Natasha. "Next time I'll forego the hug when I'm working."

"You did at least bring a suit?"

I sighed. "Yes. But really, what do they care what I wear? They just want to check I'm still working away. Which I could do a lot better if I was back in my workshop."

She went quiet.

"*What?*" I asked, dreading the answer.

"You may have to give a little presentation. Just a teensy one."

I slumped back in my seat and cursed her under my breath.

***

The "teensy" presentation turned out to be a four hour show-and-tell, with Carol doing the smarming and me on hand to answer the technical questions. They were more interested in what the missile would be able to do rather than how it worked. Lucky, because I still hadn't figured that out, and I knew I wouldn't until I was back in the workshop watching Natasha again.

I sighed and resisted the urge to close my eyes and doze off. I was sitting at the conference table while Carol wrapped up our presentation, wowing the suits with talk of casualty projections. Next, there'd be a buffet lunch and then I'd have to sit politely while someone talked about their new aircraft for four hours. Then an evening of TV in my hotel room—it was either that or go out drinking with the suits—and then the whole thing again the next day, and the next day, and the next....

A little voice told me that I'd been on these trips plenty of times before, and they'd never seemed quite this boring. Talking about my work had even been kind of fun, after months spent alone in the workshop. This time, though....

This time it was different. This time I'd seen an alternative. Natasha.

I thought of her, pirouetting smoothly on the stage, flowing from one position to the next with a lightness that didn't seem possible. The way she'd move slowly and then explode into a run, or how she'd jump and catch her balance like a cat...she made it seem so effortless. I remembered the way her hair blazed and shone when the light hit it. And when she smiled—especially if it seemed like she was smiling because she saw me—it made something swell up inside me, like—

"Interesting." A deep rumble behind me. I turned to see the white-haired CEO of the company standing there. The meeting had broken for lunch while I'd been daydreaming and people were milling around. For some reason, he was looking down at the notepad I had in front of me. I looked too.

We both stared at the full-page sketch of a ballerina. I hadn't even been aware of drawing it.

***

That afternoon, I sat near the back and tried to figure out what to text to Natasha. I wanted to let her know I was thinking of her, but I didn't want to come over as creepy, or weird. We'd only seen each other a few times, after all, and that had been business. Well, mostly business.

I had to be charming, but flirty.

But not seedy.

But interested.

But not pushy.

I sighed. *How can it be this hard?* It had always

been easy with the society women I'd dated...somehow, I'd never worried about what they thought of me. With Natasha, that was all I thought about.

Eventually, I settled on: "Thinking of you."

I didn't hear back for an hour. Then: "Thinking of you too."

I looked to the front of the room. They were talking about how their new fighter jet maneuvered—exactly the sort of thing that would have had me in rapt attention a week ago. Now it just seemed...flat.

I texted back: *"How's your day been?"* That was okay, right? Friendly but open-ended.

A minute later: *"Rehearsal. Modern class. Going to take a shower now."*

Right then, Fenbrook was the most interesting place in the world. I wanted to know everything. What was she rehearsing? Modern? Modern what? Modern history? Did they take other classes as well as dancing and stuff? Or was modern a dance style? I'd have loved to watch her dance modern. Actually, I realized, I'd have happily watched her dance the damn Macarena. And the shower comment...I knew that had been completely innocent, but it kicked off all kinds of thoughts.

I waited until I thought she'd be out of the shower—a few minutes was enough, right?—and then texted: *"Good shower?"* Immediately, I regretted it. That was too flirty.

Minutes ticked by. No reply. Five minutes. Ten.

"Very good thank you ;)" came back. She was flirting with me. Then, a few minutes later: *"Off to Harper's now."*

Who was Harper? A girl? A guy? Was it some guy's house? I thought of her going to some open house college party with kegs of beer and chisel-jawed actors, while I was stuck in Virginia. I didn't want to go overboard on the texts, so I sat there and stewed for a while and then, while I should have been listening to some guy talk about jet thrust, I found http://fenbrookacademy.com on my phone and discovered under *Life at Fenbrook* that Harper's was a coffee shop, and that made me feel a little better.

How was she doing this to me? I didn't remember when I'd been this wrapped up in a girl. I wasn't sure I'd *ever* been this wrapped up in a girl.

***

The next day, Tuesday, I couldn't concentrate at all. I texted her again, but she was in class or at rehearsals most of the day so replies came slowly and I didn't want her to think I was stalking her. By the end of the day I was mentally worn out and physically jumpy. I was used to working with my hands, feeling comfortably worn out at the end of the day. Nine hours in a conference room chair didn't agree with me.

I hit the hotel gym and heaved dumbbells until my muscles burned. It felt good, but it didn't feel satisfying like it should have done. I felt like I was hungry, but not for food. Like—

Like I missed her.

That was ridiculous. I'd seen her on Friday—it had only been four days! And yet—

The door crashed open and Carol strutted in, in designer workout gear and drinking from a water bottle that looked like it belonged in an art gallery. "Really?" I asked her. "I can't even be alone *here?*"

"I didn't come here for you," she said with a sniff. "I came here to run." And she stepped onto a treadmill and cranked it up to a jog.

For a few minutes, I lifted and she ran in blissful

silence. Of course, it was too good to last.

"I need you up early tomorrow," she told me over the expensive whir of the treadmill belt.

Her tone sounded warning bells in my head. "Why?"

She was silent.

"Where are we going?" I pressed.

She looked round at me and smiled. Realization dawned and I let the dumbbells crash to the ground, drawing angry looks from people around me. "No!"

"You'll enjoy it. You always liked the Starbucks there...."

"Damnit, Carol, why didn't you tell me?"

"Would you have come to Virginia if I had?"

I stormed out.

***

The annoying thing was, as I sat there in the sun on Wednesday lunchtime, sipping an iced mocha latte, it *was* kind of fun. Just a little bit.

"I told you you'd enjoy it," Carol reminded me from behind her huge sunglasses. "Who wouldn't like this?" She indicated the sunshine, the happy office workers relaxing around us, and the five towering walls that surrounded the plaza.

Maybe for the thousands of people who worked there, it was normal—maybe they didn't even think about it. But I'd only visited twice before and I still got a kick out of...well, just *being at the Pentagon*.

"Maybe you could get your ballerina a pen," Carol told me, sucking Frappuccino from her straw. "They have a gift shop."

I smiled. Bringing Natasha a gift *would* be cool. It would be nice, to share a little of my world with her—the cool part. I pulled out my phone and typed a text to her: *"Guess where I am?"*

A few moments later, as we finished our drinks, a reply. *"Where?"*

And then I froze, my thumbs hovering over the phone. *What was I doing?* How in hell was I going to explain being at the Pentagon? As soon as I said it, she'd know I worked in defense. Then she'd want to know what I made for them....

Something knotted in my stomach. The last thing I wanted to do was to lie to her, but.... I typed out: *"Drinking Starbucks in the sun."* Which must have seemed like the lamest reply ever.

"Come on," said Carol, taking my drink before I'd finished it. "We have a general to meet."

Part of me wondered if I was being stupid. Maybe Natasha wouldn't care. Maybe she'd be just fine with me making weapons. But deep inside, I knew that wasn't the case and not just because I was getting to know her. It was because I was starting, very slowly to look at what I did in a different way—an outsider's way—and I didn't like what I saw.

***

That afternoon, when my part of the briefing was done and Carol was telling the military about how this latest design would be *faster, more efficient, more lethal,* I opened up my laptop and started browsing the internet. I wanted to get Natasha a gift, to make up for lying to her even though she was oblivious to it. A dress for our date would be perfect...except I had no idea where to start. Sleeves or no sleeves? Long skirt? Short skirt? I could at least guesstimate her size, after studying her so closely while she danced, but in terms of women's fashion I was shooting blind. I knew what *I* thought looked good, but that was it.

I knew my limits. That night, I drafted in two female hotel receptionists and let them argue over which of my shortlist they liked best, then picked the one they settled on. When the confirmation finally popped saying the dress was on its way to Natasha's apartment, I felt slightly better.

I couldn't wait to see her again.

CHAPTER FIFTEEN

Natasha

I T WAS ONLY THURSDAY and I missed him—a lot. It took me a while to admit it to myself, but I got there in the end.

He'd texted the first day. I still wasn't sure about the winking smiley I'd sent with the text about taking a shower—had that been too much? Then a few days later, there'd been a cute text about him drinking Starbucks in the sun. I loved the fact he got a kick out of doing something simple. It made me want to sit out in the sun somewhere with him—Central Park, maybe. Listening to Karen's quartet play, nestled up against him on the grass, sounded a lot like perfection.

I was jerked out of my daydream by my phone ringing. Not a text but an actual call, and his name was on the screen. It was after six—maybe he was done with work for the day.

I sat up on my bed. "Hi." It was the first time we'd ever spoken on the phone, and it made me more excited than it really should have.

"Hi, Natasha." The sound of him saying it made

me smile. "Where are you?"

"At home. Quiet night in. How's Virginia?"

There was a pause. "Dull," he said eventually, and it sounded like he was surprised by his own answer. "I wanted to ask you something."

"Shoot."

"Will you dance for me?"

I blinked. "You mean: when you get back?"

"I mean: right now. Got Skype?"

I looked across the room to my aging laptop. It was hunk of junk compared to Clarissa's wafer-thin model, but it worked. "Yes...." I said doubtfully.

"Will you do it?" He paused. "I mean, obviously I'll pay you...."

"You don't have to pay me," I said quickly. And then realized that that pretty much amounted to a *yes*.

Why was I so hesitant? What bothered me about the idea? I mean, it seemed a little crazy, but so did dancing for a millionaire in the first place. Was it the thought of performing on camera, like some borderline-prostitute cam girl? Ridiculous. It was dancing, not sex.

"Okay," I told him, and gave him my Skype address. He called, and suddenly I could see him. *Ohmygod he looks good in a suit!* His hair was sort of tousled, as if he'd been running his hands through it, and I longed to do the same. Those perfect blue eyes were staring straight back at the screen, almost as if—

Oh yeah. He *could* see me. I looked down at myself: a t-shirt and jeans, the minimal make-up I'd worn for class and bare feet. Not great, but it could have been worse.

"Is that your hotel?" I asked, looking at the huge bed behind him.

He nodded. "Want to see?" And he turned his laptop slowly around, giving me the tour. It was a suite, with its own lounge and dining areas and a huge bathroom. It was several steps above any hotel room I'd ever stayed in, even if looked more business than romantic.

"Yours looks more interesting," he told me. "Nice bike."

I looked over my shoulder so fast I almost gave myself whiplash, taking in the hulking great exercise bike in the center of the room, the unmade bed, the washing on the floor. Now I realized why I'd been hesitant about doing this: he was getting a glimpse into my personal world. The weird thing was that even though it made me a little nervous, it didn't feel anywhere near as bad as I would have thought. It actually felt kind of good, that he was seeing the real me—or at least some of me. If I'd had time to think about it properly beforehand, I probably would have said no, but having done it I was glad I'd agreed.

"I like riding it," I told him, and then wanted to kick myself because that sounded so stupid. "When I'm riding it, I'm just doing that, you know? It helps me forget stuff." *Careful!*

But he just nodded as if he understood. "It's building things, for me."

We just looked at each other for a second, realizing that maybe we were more alike than either of us had suspected.

"So. How do we do this?" I looked around. "There's not a lot of room."

He nodded. "I'll be happy with whatever you can do."

I found some slow and tranquil music online and was about to hit "Play" when I realized I was still in a t-shirt and jeans. Combats I could dance in, but jeans were impossible. I'd have to get changed.

"Umm. Hang on a sec," I told him.

"What's up?"

What was the thing to do here? Go to the bathroom and come back? That seemed rude. But I couldn't just strip off in front of him, or this really was going to feel like some webcam sex thing....

...the idea of which didn't completely fill me with horror.

"I'm just going to put something over the camera while I change," I told him. I found a black t-shirt, thick enough to be opaque, and draped it over the top of my laptop. "There. Can you see?"

"Not a thing."

"Really?"

"Completely blind."

I put my hands on the hem of my t-shirt...and then, still shy, I turned my back to the screen. I pulled off my shirt and jeans and got into tights and a leotard. Only then did I turn back.

The t-shirt was lying on the keyboard, having slithered down at some point. Darrell was looking right into my eyes.

"When did that happen?" I asked lightly.

"Seconds ago," he deadpanned.

I just stared at him, a dark heat building inside me.

"I averted my eyes," he told me.

I was pretty sure he was lying, which only made me hotter. God, how did he do this to me? I wondered if it was the same for Clarissa, with Neil. To cover my embarrassment, I sat down and strapped on my pointe shoes.

"Does it hurt?" he asked me. "I mean, going up on pointe. It looks like it hurts."

I shook my head. "Not really. Tiring, not painful."

I stood up and started the music.

There wasn't a lot of room, so I focused on my arms—slow, measured sweeps that took me from bras bas to second to fifth. I leaned forward into third arabesque, one leg up behind me. The floor was wood, and glossy enough that I managed a promenade, rotating on one leg as I had in the park. Part of me still only wanted him to see the perfect stuff—the perfect me. But as I danced for him in that messy room, my outstretched foot inches from an exercise bike, things started to change. I stopped thinking about impressing him and started just doing it because it gave him pleasure. I came up on pointe and then sank down into a plié, and I was close enough to the screen that I could look him in the eye as I did it, watching him watch me. I formed a wide "n", lower legs vertical and calves horizontal and straining.

"You're beautiful," he said, and it was so out of nowhere that I wobbled. "Sorry," he said quickly. "But you are."

I flushed, unsure what to say. I wanted to tell him how much I loved his eyes, or the softness of his hair. But I just sort of nodded awkwardly. And going through my mind was, *You think that because you don't know me.*

But he was getting to know me. I'd wondered before if he felt the same way and now the texts and this call had given me my answer. He really did like me, maybe just as much as I liked him. Maybe more than "liked". This was going beyond just physical attraction, now. This was getting into serious territory—seriously exciting and a serious risk of him finding out about me.

I rose up out of the plié before my legs collapsed, and as the music ended, I leaned forward, closer and closer to the screen. We both had the same idea at the same time. We didn't actually kiss the screen—we stopped just short of it, with our eyes closed and our lips slightly parted—but it felt like we kissed.

"I can't wait for Monday," he told me. "I'm sorry I had to go away."

"Me too."

We talked about the date. Dinner at a fancy restaurant I hadn't heard of. A drink first at a bar I definitely had—the same one celebrities were photographed in, in all the glossy magazines.

And then what? Back to the mansion? Back here? A demure kiss on the cheek? Would it count as our first date, and sex would be too much, or were we technically on our third now?

I said goodbye and ended the call, then sat there staring at the screen. Monday still seemed like a month away, and with every day, the feelings grew more solid, more real. Being apart only seemed to make it more intense—what the hell did *that* mean? That this was the real thing? Or that I was setting myself up for some huge disappointment when he returned?

***

The next day when I got back from classes, Mr. Kresinski had taken in a package for me. When I stripped off the outer paper, I found a gold and green box with the black lettering of some store I'd never heard of.

The printed note said, *"For you to wear on Monday."*

Inside the box was a dress so beautiful I caught my breath.

It was a cocktail dress in some soft, red fabric that

seemed to flow over my fingers when I handled it. The skirt looked like it would reach down to just above the knee. It had a halter neck and a neckline that was sexy, but not over-the-top. It was...*elegant*. I didn't have anything that was elegant. I'd have to put my hair up.

I slipped out of my clothes and tried it on. He'd got the size right...but given how closely he'd been watching me, that didn't surprise me. I'd been right about the neckline. There was some cleavage on display, but it was the right side of sexy.

The skirt, though.... I looked at my legs in the mirror. It wasn't like my legs were bad—several hours of dancing a day has its benefits—but I wasn't used to seeing them bare. I either wore tights thick enough to hide the dressings I used on my scars, or pants. The skirt hid the scars fine, but I was very aware that underneath it, my thighs were bare. I'd just have to be careful.

I saw that I'd have to take the dressing off: the dress kept clinging to the edges of it. Luckily, I'd cut very little that week—just once, on Tuesday morning, after a nightmare had left me shaky. If I could manage to hold off until Monday, the cuts would be healed enough that I could get away without a dressing. Darrell would never know.

***

On Monday night, Clarissa helped me pin my hair up. I wished I had some jewelry that would look sensible with it, but everything I owned looked cheap and tacky next to the expensive fabric. I went easy on the make-up—I didn't usually wear much, unless I was on stage. Clarissa pressed me to put on more.

"I don't want to go over the top," I'd told her.

"It's a date with a millionaire, in a cocktail dress.

I've heard of that restaurant. You have to book a table *now* if you want your grandkids to eat there. It's not possible to be over the top."

I grudgingly spent a bit more time on my eyes and lips. When I came out of my room again and Clarissa saw the whole thing—dress, hair, make-up and my best pair of heels—she squealed.

"Don't," I told her. "I'm nervous enough."

"Pfft. What's the worst that could happen?"

***

Clarissa asked if I wanted company until Darrell arrived, but it wasn't as if I was going to some dive bar. This was K35, a place so painfully cool and horrendously expensive I'd never so much as dreamed of going. Okay, maybe dreamed. Besides, I trusted him to be on time—he'd said he'd be there at eight.

Just to be sure, though, I timed the cab to get me there at a few minutes past. As I opened the door and stepped out, the dress making luxuriously soft little sounds as it brushed against my legs, I felt at least eighty percent like a movie star. I walked up the curving white staircase, feeling the glances of envious tourists as the doorman held the door for me.

I wasn't quite ready for the wall of sound and the warm press of bodies that greeted me. I'm not sure what I'd been expecting—people lounging on cushions and harp music, perhaps—but it seemed that the rich scrummed around the bar just like the rest of us. I could feel the panic rising in my chest as I felt eyes on me, a million strangers who might suddenly see me for what I really was—a pretender, a shell. What I'd done burned inside me like white-hot lava. Surely everyone could see it?

Calm down. Find Darrell.

I gritted my teeth and pushed through the crowd to the bar. Thankfully, a large crowd chose that moment to move away from the bar and there was suddenly some air. A few bar stools even opened up...but there was no sign of Darrell.

I checked my watch: five past eight. He was probably stuck in traffic. OK, fine. I was a big girl. I'd sit at the bar for a minute until he arrived.

Maybe eight seconds after I sat down on a stool, a guy slid in between the stools and stood next to me. Thirties, with straw-colored hair that was already starting to thin. "Hi! Buy you a drink?"

I forced my best smile. "I'm fine, thank you. I'm waiting for someone."

He grinned and made no move to leave, so I whipped my phone out and called Darrell. I could chat to him until his cab arrived.

His phone went straight to voicemail. Why would he have it turned off? I tried not to let my disquiet come through in my voice. "Hi, it's Natasha. I'm at the bar. Just checking in." Then I couldn't think of anything else to say, so I hung up.

"Natasha. That's a beautiful name." The blond guy was still there, and apparently, he'd been listening in.

I gave him a tight little smile and then looked away.

"Come on, let me buy you a drink while you wait for him. Hey!" The last was to the barman, who sauntered over. "I'll have another one of these. Natasha, what do you want?"

He'd obviously read some dating guide that said using a girl's name would make her feel close to him, or special, or more likely to drop her panties or something.

"I'll have a cranberry juice—*I'll* pay, thank you."

"With a shot of vodka in it, and *I'll* pay," said the blond man.

"*No* shot, *thank you.*" My voice was icily cold. The barman nodded and walked off and the blond man sighed and went back to his friends.

Ten minutes later, I'd gone through most of my cranberry juice, clutching the glass so tightly my fingers had gone numb from its chill. Where *was* he? I was starting to get mad at him, which at least pushed back my panic a little. I pulled out my phone and dialed him. Voicemail again. "Hi, me again. Everything okay? It's eight fifteen." And then, because I could see the blond guy coming back, I added, "You're late!"

I hung up and concentrated intently on my phone, scrolling through old text messages and hoping that would keep him at bay. It didn't.

"If I dated you, I wouldn't keep you waiting."

I turned to look at him. "You aren't dating me."

"Ooh. Ouch. But I could be. I'm Rick."

I just looked at him.

"And you're Natasha. Are you a model, Natasha?"

I'd had guys come onto me plenty of times before. It didn't make me panic, as long as I could get up and leave. That was the problem—I was waiting for Darrell, so I couldn't.

He moved in closer to me, but it wasn't the closeness. It was the attention. He thought I was beautiful, or at least attractive, and that only made me more aware of the secret I was hiding—the ugliness of what I'd done. Why didn't Darrell do this to me? Why did his gaze on me feel good, when everyone else's felt bad? The feelings weren't made any better by the knowledge that I was several social strata below everyone else in the bar.

"Really, it's not a line," he insisted. "Are you a model? You have fantastic legs."

I thought of the scars, right there under the loose fabric, almost on show. "Thank you," I replied, realizing too late that it would only encourage him. That he'd think my blushing was embarrassment at the compliment, a signal for him to proceed.

One of his friends called to him, and he gestured angrily to them, nodding at me. He thought he was going to get lucky. Thankfully, they managed to draw him away, but he made *I'll be right back* gestures.

I checked my watch. Eight twenty-five. *Where was he?* I was too scared to be angry now, dangerously close to panic. What if something had happened to him? God, I'd been so selfish, worrying about sitting in a bar with some annoying jerk. What if his limo had crashed? What if he'd had some accident in the workshop? I pulled out my phone and got his voicemail *again.* "Darrell, I'm worried"—my voice caught and I had to force myself to relax. "Call me, okay? Call me now."

As soon as I put the phone down, everything seemed to close in around me. Everyone was suddenly standing too close and it was far, far too hot. I could see the blond guy coming back. He'd seen me hang up the phone again and I could tell what he was thinking. I'd been stood up. I was easy pickings.

He's right. You have been stood up. My stomach churned. *What did you expect? Did you think it was real? Did you think it would last?*

The floor started to slide and tilt. I had to grab hold of the bar top, dig my fingers into its hardness. My brain started to scream, over and over, the one thought that until now I'd been too terrified to even entertain....

He's found out.

The blond guy was back and this time he actually

sat down beside me, shifting his bar stool towards mine as he did so. His leg pressed against mine, and I was too focused on trying not to cry to pull away.

Of course, he took that as a sign of acceptance.

"So. Natasha. I don't think your guy's coming. He's an asshole. Come on, a drink. Nothing more."

I didn't respond. I was staring straight ahead, trying to fight my way up out of the memories, but it was like being sucked down into thick, dark treacle.

He took my silence as passivity. "Unless you *want* something more. Maybe you do." His voice seemed to come from the other end of a long, dark tunnel, yet I could feel his mouth right up against my ear. "Maybe you're one of those women who like to be told what to do."

His hand was on my thigh.

I scrambled off my stool and ran, blundering through the crowd on legs that threatened to collapse under me at any second.

Of course he doesn't want you. Nobody wants you. You were fooling them and they found out. They know what you are.

I saw the sign for the restrooms. Nothing felt real or substantial anymore, except the hard lines of the cigarette case as I pulled it from my handbag.

CHAPTER SIXTEEN

Darrell
Two hours earlier

THE ALARM WENT OFF, but I ignored it.

I was at the whiteboard and lost in theories and equations, trying to catch up after a full week wasted in Virginia. I knew I was close. I kept imagining Natasha, doing her fouettés and pirouettes, or doing the promenade in her bedroom, spinning slowly without any apparent effort....

My phone beeped. Not an alarm, this time. A text message from Carol: "*Back at work, I hope. Not having private dances?*" I sighed and ignored her. A few moments later, another message: "*Seriously, are you on the job, or on the ballerina?*" I slammed the phone down without replying.

The second alarm—the one I'd set because I knew I'd ignore the first one—went off. I silenced it and grinned as I thought about seeing Natasha. I really had to go and get ready, or I'd be late to meet her. I needed to shower, find a shirt, get my suit on....

Another text message arrived from Carol: "*Are you ignoring me?*"

I viciously stabbed the power button and held it down until the screen went black.

In blissful silence, I took one last look at the whiteboard. I had to make it move like Natasha moved...

Natasha. The irony was, the more I thought about her, the more I was inspired by her, the less comfortable I was with the project. I ran my hand over the casing. It was the best—or the worst—I'd ever built. And once I cracked the problem, its most deadly ability would come directly from her, from her dancing. She was going to be the inspiration for something that destroyed cities...countries.

Neil would say to walk away from the whole thing, but then he didn't understand why I did it in the first place. He didn't know what was driving me, deep down—no one did, except Carol. And I knew I wasn't going to open myself up enough to explain it to Natasha, either. Without even realizing it, I was tracing my scars through my vest, and just the thought of that day roused the memories from their slumber. I remembered then why I didn't let myself question my work, but it was too late.

I quickly turned on some music and cranked the volume up loud. I could feel a cold sweat breaking out across my back as the screams filled my ears, the music failing to block them out. The anger rose up inside me like a physical force, every muscle going tense. I picked up the whiteboard marker, but my hand was shaking so hard I could barely write. I wanted to scream and yell and hurl stuff around the room, but smashing up my workshop would be letting *them* win.

Work, that was the answer. Solve the problem.

Build the weapon. Use my rage. I took a deep breath and started to work through equations on the whiteboard, knuckles white on the pen, hoping, *praying* that if I focused hard enough the memories would sink back down.

Slowly—very slowly—it worked.

....

When I reached for my Dr. Pepper, I noticed it was warm. Weird...I'd only taken it from the cooler a few....

Oh God! It was eight thirty! I was supposed to have met Natasha a half hour ago, and I wasn't even in the city yet!

I ran for the elevator.

***

Five minutes later, after the shortest shower in history, I exploded out of the front door of the mansion in just my jockey shorts. The driver was waiting patiently in the car—he would have waited all night, if he'd had to. I wrenched open the rear door and threw the armful of clothes I was carrying inside and then dived in after it.

I gave the driver the address of the bar and told him there was an extra hundred in it for him if he got us there before nine. As we sped down the highway, I tried to pull my pants on with one hand while I scrambled for my phone to call Natasha. Why hadn't she called me? She must have been livid....

My heart sank as I saw the black screen of my phone and remembered turning it off. When I fired it up, I had three missed calls, all from Natasha.

Helena Newbury

CHAPTER SEVENTEEN

Natasha

I STAGGERED INTO THE RESTROOM, glimpsing slate tiles and soft, subdued lighting before I crashed into a stall and slammed the door. I pulled the dress up around my hips and sat down, my breath coming in quick, high gasps. The scars were so old, so well-healed, and that only made it worse. I hadn't cut in six days, the longest I'd managed in a year or more, and I was about to destroy it all.

My hands were shaking so much I dropped the first blade. I pulled out the second and held it against my thigh. For a second, I caught a glimpse of my own reflection in its shining surface, saw my red eyes and mascara tears. I hadn't even realized I'd started to cry.

The edge of the blade caught my thigh. A slight friction and the soft compression of my pale skin—

My phone rang.

I grabbed it with my free hand. The screen told me it was Darrell calling, but I didn't answer, just sat there frozen, blade in one hand and phone in the other. Two rings. Three. Hot tears dripped onto my bare legs. The blade changed from cold to warm as it nestled against my skin.

I looked between my hands. I needed something to cling onto. Something real.

I pressed the button.

"Natasha! I am so, so sorry! Natasha?"

I swallowed, tasting saltwater. "Yes," I whispered.

His voice changed immediately. "Are you okay?"

I sniffed loudly and I could hear the pain in his voice when he spoke again. "Natasha I am *so* sorry. I'm coming, I'll be there in no time at all!"

I took a shuddering breath. I didn't trust myself to speak.

He stayed on the line, offering reassurance and apologies, and I wanted to be okay for him, to dry my tears and laugh and joke, but I just couldn't. And he knew I couldn't—I could hear the fear in his voice.

And then suddenly I could hear his voice through the door, and I gasped and sniffed and stuffed the blades into the cigarette case and then I was opening the door and he was clasping me close to his chest as I sobbed into his shoulder.

"It's okay," he told me, and he repeated it over and over until it was.

I thought of the people outside, the crowd who'd seen me stagger into the restroom. "I don't want to stay here," I told him.

He nodded immediately and, slipping an arm around my waist, led me out of the restroom and towards the door. I kept my head down, my cheeks still shining with tears.

A man in a suit loomed ahead of us. Blond hair. Rick.

"Good luck, man," he said as we passed. "She's a fuckin' psycho."

Darrell whirled and slugged the guy, drawing a scream from a woman nearby. The man careened backwards, knocking over two of his friends. He didn't get up.

Darrell gently escorted me outside. There was a Mercedes there, with the engine running and the door already open.

"Will you let me take you somewhere else?" he asked.

I stared at him for a long moment, and then nodded.

***

We sped past two blocks before anyone spoke. The car was so thickly insulated the city outside barely existed—just a fantasy, a movie projected onto the windows.

The driver discreetly asked a question and Darrell told him, "Just drive around."

He sat sideways on the cream leather so he could look at me. I knew I looked a complete mess, but just having him close was already calming me. My worst fears were being pushed back. He didn't know. Of course he didn't know. He couldn't know, or he wouldn't still want me in his life. There was still hope.

Except...now he must think I was a complete psycho, just like that guy had said.

"I'm really sorry," he told me.

I didn't know what to say.

"Please, Natasha. Talk to me."

You mean explain why you completely freaked out, just because I was late.

"Where were you?" I said at last. I didn't mean it as an accusation, but immediately I could see the guilt on his face. I'm good at recognizing guilt, because I'm so good at hiding it. "What?" He closed his eyes. "What? What happened?"

He still had his eyes closed. I could tell he was fighting with himself, wanting to tell me the truth despite what the consequences would be. "I...forgot."

"You...*forgot?*"

I'd run through all sorts of scenarios while I'd been sitting in the bar. A flat tire. An accident on the highway. A dying grandmother. He *forgot?* I was that unimportant to him?

He opened his eyes and looked straight at me, his hands in the air, trying to tame the outburst he could see was coming. "I get...kind of...*into* my work, sometimes. Sort of obsessed. I forgot the time."

I couldn't believe what I was hearing. I was less important than his work? "But...your phone was off."

He closed his eyes as he said it, wincing, "...I didn't want to be disturbed."

"I was calling you," I said, my voice lifeless and dull. "I was calling you and calling you. We were meant to be on a *date—*"

"I know—"

"But you didn't want to be *disturbed?*"

"Natasha, I know. I'm sorry." He grabbed my hand and held it, the warmth from his huge palms slowly soaking into me. "I messed up. I *really* messed up and, look—" He locked eyes with me. "It will never. Happen. Again. I swear." And those eyes, those beautiful calm blue pools that took away all my fear...they allowed me to hope. I still didn't understand how he could have put his work before me, if he really liked me. It still hurt. But the connection, the magic between us...that was back.

I nodded, and saw him relax just a little.

"I'm sorry I upset you." He was looking at me with real worry in his eyes. I didn't want to think about how I must look, or what I'd sounded like on the phone.

"It wasn't...." I had to explain, somehow, without letting him know too much. I couldn't let him think he was solely responsible. "It's not all you," I told him at last.

He nodded, and in his eyes, I saw that it was okay. And something else, too, something I wasn't expecting. A sort of surprised understanding, as if my weirdness was the last thing he was expecting, but that it wasn't totally unfamiliar. How could that be? He was everything I wasn't: stable, rich and a goddamn genius. His only weirdness was that he was interested in me.

He leaned forward and gently rested his forehead against mine. It felt good.

"Some date, huh?" he murmured, and even though my eyes were still damp, I sort of laughed.

"I can drop you at your place," he told me gently. "Or...if you want to...we could give this another go?"

I wanted to. But..."I don't think I can face a restaurant," I told him.

He nodded. "Me neither." He took a deep breath. "Pizza?"

***

We stopped at some place he knew, not a franchise but a tiny brick building with a faded sign and an aging, Italian owner who came out to meet us. We waited in the car, my back snuggled into his chest, until the driver returned with a huge, steaming box that he slid onto the seat next to us, its warmth filling the car.

Back at the mansion, Darrell ordered me out of

the dining room while he got it ready. "Let me at least try to make this back into a date," he insisted.

I wanted to do something about my face, and went off to find a bathroom. It was the first time I'd seen the rest of the house. On the second floor alone, there were a bewildering number of doors, but as I pushed open one after another I found most of the rooms were unused, the beds not made up.

I figured I should use the bathroom in *his* bedroom, because that would have towels and things. It wasn't just about satisfying my curiosity. At least, that's what I told myself.

In the end, it wasn't hard to work out which bedroom he slept in. It was the nearest one to the staircase—his male mind at work—and the only one that looked remotely lived in. There was a massive four-poster bed, a half-open closet and, in one corner, a mirror with some photos around the edge. Apart from the workshop, they seemed to be the only personal touch in the whole house.

I stepped closer. Was this invading his privacy? I glanced at the door, but I could hear him still busy downstairs....

Some of the photos were from his college days at MIT. I recognized Neil, long-haired and bearded even then. There were other drinking buddies, the rowing team and some sort of fraternity. The photos seemed to be in chronological order, from freshman to sophomore...and then there was an abrupt change. After that, there were only photos like the one Clarissa had shown me online, of Darrell shaking hands with people in suits. One woman—a worryingly pretty, dark-haired woman a good ten years older than me—seemed to be in every one of them. Even through the posed smiles, I could see the way she was looking at Darrell.

There was a noise from downstairs and I ran for the bathroom before I got caught. Standing at the sink, I repaired the worst of the damage and then gripped the cold porcelain for strength. *You can do this.*

A moment later I walked lightly down the stairs and into the dining room...then stopped abruptly in the doorway.

A long table that would have seated twenty was set for just the two of us, and Darrell had gone all out. There were snow-white cloth napkins, crystal wine glasses and a bottle of champagne sweating in an ice bucket. And then, right in the middle, there was the still-steaming pizza box.

It was absurd, and perfect. Except...he'd added one more touch, in a bid to be romantic, and it had me paralyzed in the doorway.

He smiled at me, oblivious, and walked around to my side to pull my chair out for me.

I took a deep breath. *Just get through it.* I sat down.

"You look beautiful," he told me as he sat down across from me, but his voice seemed to come from far away. I could feel myself sliding, as if my chair was plunging down towards the memories.

Focus. Under the table, I dug my nails into my palms. I thanked him—I think—I honestly can't remember what I said.

They were drawing my eyes. I tried to look at Darrell, to lose myself in those gorgeous blue pools, but it was as if I was hypnotized. My skin was crawling, my stomach churning. I couldn't breathe.

Darrell's mouth was moving, but I couldn't hear. There was a noise in my ears. Screaming. My screaming, from that night—

I stood up, my chair shrieking as it scraped across

the floor.

Darrell rose slowly, confused. "Are you okay?"

I swallowed, feeling sick and terrified and completely humiliated. "Can we not have them?" I asked.

He looked blankly at me. His eyes were full of concern—he was desperately trying to understand. "What?"

Of course. They were so dominating my mind, it hadn't occurred to me that he'd have no idea what was scaring me. *That's because he's normal and you're a freak,* I thought bitterly.

"The candles," I told him weakly.

He blinked a couple more times and then quickly blew them out. Then he picked up the candelabra and carried it out of the room.

When he returned, the fear was dying away and I was left shaky and hugely embarrassed. *Twice in one night.*

"I'm sorry," he told me.

"Not your fault." I took a deep breath and tried to change the subject. Part of me wanted to tell him, then, but there was just no way I could. I liked him; I wanted him to like me. I managed to look him in the eye and he looked so worried that I cursed myself, while at the same time wanting to just leap across the table and hug him for being so patient and understanding. He was desperate to know what was going on with me, I realized, but he wouldn't ask. The trust he had in me...it made me go weak.

Maybe, given time, if I could find the right way of telling him....

"Champagne?" he raised the bottle.

"God, yes." I passed him my glass.

I wasn't a big wine drinker—it was either vodka with Clarissa or the occasional cocktail with Jasmine, if anything at all. But the champagne was different to anything I'd had before. It wasn't the cheap fizz I'd had at weddings. It had real taste and the bubbles were sharp and perfect. All of the waffle people talked about wine, about hints of grapefruit and summers days—that all suddenly made sense. It was the same kind of revelation a driver would have, if he'd only ever known a Ford Pinto and you sat him in a Ferrari. Sipping it gave me time to recover.

"Okay?" he asked. And I knew he wasn't just asking about the wine.

I nodded. With the candles gone, I could feel my body slowing down, all the adrenaline draining away. My face was still hot with humiliation. I had to get him talking about something else.

"Neil," I said. "Tell me about Neil."

He smirked and opened the pizza box. The smell of crisp pepperoni and melted cheese hit us. "Wondering if Clarissa's safe?"

"Wondering if Neil's safe. Clarissa takes no prisoners."

"I met him in college—we roomed together, actually." He passed me a slice of pizza. "He was sort of a hippy even back then. The biker part...that came later." He was staring into his champagne glass now, remembering. "I was a little...intense, after my folks died. I was already working on my first design, and it got a little...." He trailed off. "Neil watched out for me."

I smiled. "He doesn't seem like an MIT graduate." I bit into the pizza and it was fantastically good, the base delicately crunchy and the sauce tangy and rich. Gooey cheese and thick, salty slices of pepperoni. Heaven.

"More than a graduate. He's still there, you know. Post-grad, doing his doctorate. Another few years—"

"It'll be *Doctor* Neil?"

"Doctor Neil, PhD in advanced aerospace engineering. He's talking seriously about riding the Harley up on stage to get his certificate."

"I'd like to see that." Talking to him was so *easy*. Why did the guilt drain away, whenever I was near him? Why did I feel...*normal?* "I have two more years at Fenbrook." I still didn't know exactly how old he was, and that reminded me of something else I wanted to know. "When I first came here...Neil said you didn't have your degree."

He nodded. "I dropped out."

I waited, giving him time.

He looked down at the table. "End of my sophomore year, my parents died. I started working." He met my eyes. "I mean, working a *lot*. And I wound up selling a design to Sabre and...I dropped out." He was silent for a second and then his voice changed, making light of it. "I mean, I was making good money—really good." He indicated the grand room around us. "It seemed crazy to stay on at MIT, and I figured I could always go back."

Something had happened. Not just his parents' death, awful as that must have been. Something had happened *to him,* changed him.

"You said it was a car bomb?" I wasn't sure how far I should push. "Here?"

He shook his head slowly. "Middle East."

"That must have been awful—them being so far away."

He looked at me for a second, and I thought he was going to say something else, but then he just nodded. There was something there, some horror he wasn't ready to return to.

What if he's like me?
Don't be stupid. No one's like you.

He handed me another slice of pizza. "So. Where do you hang out, when you're not dancing?" We looked at each other for a second and an understanding passed between us. We needed normality for a little while, or at least our approximation of it.

I took the slice. "Flicker. *With* an 'e'. The bar, not the photo site." And I started to tell him about Flicker and Harpers, and Jasmine and Karen. About rehearsals and classes and auditions, and why it's never a good idea to date an actor but every girl wants to anyway. He told me about the parties he went to—charity balls and opening nights, people with too much money and too much time.

"There's a party the day after tomorrow," he told me. "Twenty or thirty people. Just drinks, here at the house. Will you come? Neil and Clarissa could come too."

Just the thought of being around that many strangers, all asking questions, made my chest go tight. But I'd be with Darrell.... "That'd be fun," I told him.

We ate slowly, our eyes on each other as much as on the pizza. I kept looking at the little area of smooth, tan flesh revealed by his open collar. I wanted to know what his body looked like under that shirt.

There were a lot of silences, and somehow they weren't uncomfortable at all.

His ankle grazed my bare leg, stroking down my calf, and I caught my breath. I looked up and met his eyes as he ran his warm touch up and down my leg, every nerve ending suddenly quivering. It's amazing how sensitive a leg can be, when you're completely focused on it. With every touch, I could feel my arousal notching higher.

He asked me about being a dancer: about how we stay up on pointe, how we remember the choreography and what the male dancers are like. I asked him about building stuff: about what it's like to create something physical and lasting, about working for months or years on a single problem, about the frustration of abandoning prototype after prototype until you find the solution.

And then it went quiet and we just stared at each other.

All the fear I'd felt earlier had gone, and I was almost trembling with the feelings he was stirring up in me. When he stood up and walked around the table, I just sat staring up at him, helpless.

Everything suddenly felt different. This wasn't like being down in the workshop, with Clarissa upstairs. This was two people alone.

He pulled my chair out—not just enough for me to get out, but right back a good few feet. I sat there, frozen, my whole body singing with excitement.

He bent over me, and I looked up into his eyes. He smiled that knockout smile and I swear my heart flipped over. Then his strong hands were on my waist...I shrieked in surprise as he lifted me effortlessly up and turned me around, until I felt the hard wood of the table under my ass. He sat me there, my legs swinging free.

"Natasha...." he said. He didn't follow it with anything. It was as if he just liked saying it.

He stepped closer and I put my hands out against his chest. To stop him? To feel his body? Both, I think. I gasped at how warm he was, at the smooth curves of him, his chest like a wall. And then he was moving in, his hips pushing my knees open, and I closed my eyes as he kissed me.

The first time had been quick, the second gentle. This was urgent and barely restrained, promising much more to come. I could feel my breath starting to come in short, hot pants, our teeth clacking together for an instant as we moved into it. His tongue slipped into my mouth, searching and demanding, and mine danced with it.

His hand was on my back, pulling me to him, and the spread of his fingers made me aware of how big he was—I felt like a doll next to him. His other hand was on my hip, the warmth of it seeming to burn through the dress. I shifted my body to press against his palm and heard him groan through the kiss.

He stepped closer, pushing in between my thighs and spreading my knees, the dress riding up. His hand was sliding up my leg, up my inner thigh—

With a strangled gasp, I pulled away from him, leaning back on the table. He stepped back, but it was already too late. I knew he'd felt the scars. I'd felt his fingertips graze the rough lines.

"Did I hurt you?" he asked, panicked.

For just a second, a little voice told me to say *yes*, because that would have been an easy way out. But I couldn't do that to him. I shook my head. "No, it's..." And suddenly I was crying, because I'd blown it. He'd felt the scars and now he'd have questions I couldn't answer.

He moved in again and hugged me, and I pressed my face into his chest as I sobbed and sobbed, the sort of tears that burn as they come out. Crying didn't make me feel better, but worse. Crying was speeding me down towards the place where I'd break open and everything would come spilling out. And then I'd lose him forever.

I pushed him away again and shook my head furiously. "It's—" I was going to say "*It's nothing,*" but the look on his face told me I wasn't going to get away with that. "It's—Not something I want to talk about." I sniffed. "Is that okay?"

He nodded urgently and swept me up in his arms again. I was still sobbing, but this time it was okay because we weren't lurching towards a point where I'd have to tell him. We were moving away, back to safety, and suddenly I was furious at myself. I'd already had two freak-outs. I was damned if I was going to let a third ruin everything.

I reached up, grabbed his face between my hands and kissed him, as hard as I could. Startled, he pulled back a little, but I followed him, feeling the hot tears trickling down my face as I moved. I was still crying, saltwater on my lips as I knitted my fingers in his hair and kissed him again and again, quick and hot and urgent.

He broke away, gasping. "We don't have to—"

"I want to." And my mouth was back on his, my tongue slipping into his mouth.

He started returning the kiss, his thumbs brushing the wetness from my cheeks. I could feel my tears slowing. He slid one hand down to my bare shoulder, cupping it, and the warmth of it—so *real*—coaxed me farther from the edge, back towards safety. I twisted into the kiss, exploring his lips, the memories slithered reluctantly back into the shadows. The *now* took over, and my tears finally stopped.

His hand slid into my hair, his palm cupping my head and gently tilting it back. Then he broke the kiss, leaving me gasping as he laid a trail of kisses down my throat. I felt it start, the slow swirl of heat in my belly, like I was coming back to life. His lips moved lower, down to my chest, to the soft upper valley of my breasts, and I took a deep, long breath as the heat inside spread outwards.

He stopped for a second. Just long enough to look me in the eyes, to know that I was okay. I looked steadily back at him, my breath coming in shuddering gasps, and nodded.

His hands found my legs again, but this time he traced up the outside, over the dress, and when I didn't jerk or pull away I felt him relax. He cupped my ass, almost lifting me up off the table, and I went weak.

My hands were running down his back, marveling at the muscles there, tracing down to his waist...and then his tight, firm ass. I felt his palms slide up my back, until they reached the loop of the dress's halter neck. He pulled and it stretched, and as I ducked my head there was just enough give in the fabric to drag it over my hair and off. The fabric flopped down to my chest, and then there was nothing holding the dress up but friction.

He stroked it down with his hands, sliding the fabric over the glossy cups of my bra. His mouth returned, and this time I tangled my fingers in the soft curls of his hair as he explored their softness, tongue running over and between them until I was groaning. The heat inside me was rising, growing darker. I wanted to grind my body against him, wanted him naked against me. I grabbed the hem of his shirt and jerked it up, baring his back, and then as I pulled it higher he took over and stripped it off over his head.

Everything stopped.

Ever since I'd first fantasized about him, I'd had the mental picture of his firm, muscled abs in my head. They were just as hard and defined as I'd imagined—better, even, but—

Starting on his stomach and winding around his side, there was a sweeping constellation of brutal, jagged scars. I felt my mouth open, horrified that anyone would want to ruin his perfection. I looked up at him, and he was staring back at me. Pleading with me not to ask.

I nodded. And a little voice cruelly taunted that the wrench I felt inside, the sick fear at not knowing—that was the same experience I'd just given him.

I ran my fingers down his arms, tracing his form as if he were a statue. Then over his chest, my palms flat against the broad sweep of those delicious pecs, feeling the hardness of them. And finally, tentatively down, ready to stop if he wanted me to. I looked up into his eyes as I smoothed over the damaged skin, following the shape of it round to his side. He stared right back into my eyes and I could see the pain his memories were bringing him, but he didn't stop me.

I realized he was undoing my bra. I gasped as his fingers finished with the clasp, and then my breasts were throbbing in the cool air of the huge room. His mouth closed on one breast, tongue slathering the nipple, and as I felt it pucker and stiffen, I whispered his name.

He lifted me onto the table, on my back, a plate hitting the floor. He climbed up onto it himself, kneeling astride one of my legs. Suddenly everything was different. A minute ago, we'd been kissing. Now, we were going to....

He lowered himself atop me, moving between my legs and kissing me again, and now his naked chest was rubbing against my breasts with every movement, the sensations driving me wild, making me grind myself against the hardness I could feel at his groin.

He sat back on his haunches. My skirt was up around my thighs. He stared into my eyes as he reached up under the fabric and hooked my panties. I lifted my ass, showing my willing, and he dragged them off.

I watched him unfasten his pants and push them down. God, he was already hard and...big. He rolled a condom on, and then moved over me. And then I felt him....*God!*

I arched my back as he moved into me, hissing through my teeth at his girth, at the feeling of being filled. My breasts mashed against his chest, my hands tracing down his naked back, feeling his muscles flex as he began to move. The heat inside me bloomed and rose, claiming me for its own.

Silken hardness as he thrust. My head going back, hair tossing as he filled me again and again. My hands slid down to his ass, kneading his firm cheeks, pulling him into me, needing him. Something rolled off the table and smashed.

I started to grind back against him, the heat inside me whirling and building, out of control. The delicious tight friction of him, my legs wrapping around him as he reached a frenzy, and then I was gasping and shouting his name as I felt myself tipping over the edge. He was driving hard into me, and as my orgasm broke I closed my eyes and went rigid, wanting that moment to go on forever. The pleasure exploded inside me and I strained and shook, and before I'd recovered I felt him shudder and groan himself.

He took his weight on his arms so as not to crush me, and wrapped his arms protectively around my quaking body. I was a mess. Half-dressed, on a dining table, my mascara no doubt in long rivers down my face. But God, I felt so good.

As he got his breath back, he asked, "Would you like...to move somewhere more comfortable?" And despite everything, I giggled.

CHAPTER EIGHTEEN

Darrell

I LAY BACK ON THE BED and tried to think. So much had happened in the last half hour that it was a relief just to have a second to stop and *process*.

Thinking was difficult, though, because of what was happening not ten feet from where I was lying. When we'd come upstairs, Natasha had glimpsed herself in the mirror, seen the pizza crumbs in her hair and the long black waterfalls of mascara on her cheeks and immediately asked to take a shower. That meant she was in there naked. And wet. And slippery. And every time she moved around under the spray, I could hear the change in the sound of the water and couldn't help but imagine her lithe body twisting and bending and—

Concentrate, dammit!

I was an asshole. My work gave me a way of dealing with my memories, but it came at a cost: one that had left Natasha alone in a bar, in tears. She must have thought I was a cold, uncaring bastard. She probably

149

thought I cared more about my work than I did her, and that wasn't the case, could *never* be the case. I just—

I sighed out loud. How could I explain to her why I did it? How could I explain the anger that pulled me out of bed at three in the morning, when I woke from yet another nightmare, and sent me straight down to the workshop to hammer and weld? How could I explain the way my work made me feel? The sense of vengeance, the feeling of fighting back?

It wasn't just being obsessed with work that she'd never understand. It was what I made—instruments of death. And yet that was what made it work—that's what kept me functioning. Being able to *do* something, to take action, even at a distance...it was the only thing that made life bearable. Since I'd met Natasha, the purity of it, the certainty that I was doing the right thing, seemed a hell of a lot less clear cut. She was making me see things in a whole new light. But if I stopped making weapons, what was I supposed to do instead? Forget the past? Forget *them?*

The memories started to come back, the tang of exhaust fumes and the scrunch of sand beneath my shoes. I screwed my eyes closed and concentrated. *Focus. Stop being so selfish. Concentrate on Natasha.*

I'd reduced her to tears, three times in one night. Or I'd been the catalyst, at least, for the reawakening of some awful memory. And I knew what that was like—had felt the same thing, when the subject of my parents had come up. And again, when she'd seen my scars.

I had to figure it out. I knew that she wouldn't tell me, and I wouldn't push her for an answer. But I couldn't accept the idea of her being broken. Not my Natasha. I had to fix her, and if that meant working out what had happened to her on my own, so be it.

I sat up on the bed, staring at the door to the

bathroom. I thought back to the candles. Why would she be scared of them? I'd heard of people using them as part of sex games, dripping hot wax on each other. Had she had an abusive boyfriend—some BDSM relationship that went bad? And then there were the scars I'd felt, on her thigh.

I turned it over and over in my mind...until I remembered what she'd said when we were sitting on the edge of the stage. It had made her uncomfortable then, too. Foster care. She'd gone into foster care after her parents died.

My stomach lurched. It wasn't difficult to piece together. She'd been fifteen years old, with no one to protect her. And some guy, probably her foster dad—

I thought I was going to throw up. And then I heard her move again, behind the door, and the rage hit me. Not the slow, burning anger I lived with every day. This was fresh and ice cold, a hurricane wiping out all thought and reason. The idea that someone would hurt her, this perfect girl, break her mind and scar her body and leave her damaged. The knowledge that I hadn't been there to protect her—

The water shut off in the bathroom, and my anger hardened into resolve.

I hadn't been able to prevent it, but I could sure as hell make it right now. I'd help her, fix her. I'd find the son of a bitch who did this to her and—

She stepped out of the bathroom, her hair still wet but the dress back on. I jumped off the bed and ran to her, sweeping her up off the ground and into a hug.

She clung to me, surprised. "It's okay," she told me, feeling the tension in my body, every muscle rigid.

"It isn't," I told her. "But I'm going to make it okay, Natasha. I'm going to make everything okay."

CHAPTER NINETEEN

Natasha

H E HELD ME FOR LONG MINUTES. The shower had been glorious, the scalding water sluicing away the last traces of the dredged-up memories. When I'd emerged, wet hair still dripping, I'd felt pleasantly sleepy and warm. I'd wanted to cuddle. I hadn't been expecting a bear hug.

What's gotten into him? But I had a horrible feeling that I knew. He'd felt my scars, however briefly. Maybe he knew that I cut. But if that was true...why was he hugging me? Why wasn't he angry, or disgusted?

When he eventually released me, I looked up into his eyes. In my bare feet, he was a lot taller than me. "Darrell?"

He looked down at me with such warmth and caring that I felt a tiny shred of hope. Maybe he wasn't like everyone else. Maybe, somehow, he understood.

He pulled me close, my head on his chest. "I know," he said softly. "I know, okay?" The hope flared and shone inside. He *did* understand! I flung my arms around him and buried my face in his chest. After a moment, he gently moved me back and held me there, so he could look into my eyes. "I didn't say it before, but I've meant to—ever since I got back from Virginia—"

"What?"

"I love you."

He took my face between his hands and kissed me again and again. I managed a delighted "I love you too!" between kisses.

He led me over to the bed and we fell onto it together. He lay on his back and I slid in next to him, my head on the firm pillow of his chest. It was the closest...the *safest* I'd felt in years.

***

The next morning, it took me just a second to work out where I was. It was the first time I'd slept anywhere other than my own bed in about a year, and that *OhmyGod* moment of realizing that no, that *wasn't* my ceiling, was like an ice bath. My head was still on Darrell's chest, deliciously warm and firm, and I snuggled up against it while I remembered. The meal. The sex.

The scars. He'd felt the scars. He'd figured out that I cut myself.

But after the sickening lurch of fear, a calming warmth settled in. My second-worst fear had come to pass. He'd discovered I cut myself...but he'd been okay with it. He hadn't demanded answers or got angry with me. He'd just wrapped me up in those big arms and made me feel safe. After so many years out in the cold, I barely dared let myself hope...but maybe this was going to work out. If he was really happy not to probe further, then my worst fear—that someone would find out what I'd done—maybe that never had to happen.

I got up without waking him and crept downstairs, closing the bedroom door behind me. The night before he'd whisked me upstairs, and I hadn't really taken in just how big the sweeping oak staircase was. I padded down it barefoot, and then caught my breath as I stepped onto the freezing marble tiles of the hallway. Coffee. I needed coffee.

The kitchen was as showroom-spotless as I remembered it. I was starting to realize that he really didn't use the mansion, aside from the bedroom and bathroom. He lived in the workshop. What did he do for food? And what was it about his work that had him so caught up in it? I was still hurt that he'd put his work before me, but given what he'd just accepted about me, he deserved some leeway.

There was something else, too. I'd seen how sorry he was in the car—it was almost as if his work wasn't a choice, as if it was beyond his control. I remembered how relaxed he'd seemed, when I'd first met him and he'd declared he was an engineer. Now, every time the subject came up, he seemed tense. Was that my doing? Was I coming between him and his work, making him unhappy? Or was there something else going on?

The scars on his side. Was it all tied in with that? Sooner or later, we were going to have to talk. But I sure as hell wasn't going to push him—not when I needed to keep hold of my own secret. This whole thing felt fragile as hell, but if we nurtured it...I allowed myself a smile. Maybe, just maybe, this could work.

I thought back to the pizza. Pizza and champagne—the way he'd rescued the date had been so *him,* so spontaneous. I saw a lot of that in him: he'd needed a stage for me, so he'd just had one built the same day, right in his workshop; he'd wanted me as his muse, so he'd scoured Facebook and tracked me down; he'd wanted to see ballet, so he'd just barged into an audition.... Well, okay, so maybe barging into the audition hadn't gone so well, but if he hadn't done that, we'd never have met. I admired his confidence, his ability to just make a decision and go with it, instead of being paralyzed by every choice.

At first, I thought there wasn't any coffee, but then I found an aging, open packet with enough grounds for a couple of mugs. I smirked—he really did never use this place. By contrast, I'd seen a coffee pot in the workshop with about six different brands of coffee lined up next to it. He obviously couldn't tear himself away from his work long enough to even come upstairs.

At that moment, I heard my phone ring, the music echoing through the house. *Shit!* I didn't want to wake him. I raced in the direction of the music, the coffee packet hitting the floor behind me and coughing grounds across the tiles. I burst into the dining room, the table still littered with the detritus of the night before. *Where was it?* I listened, and eventually homed in on it: in my handbag, under the table. I knelt, cursing, scrambled through the bag, rooted out my phone and answered without looking to see who it was.

"Hello?" I was panting, pushing loose locks of hair out of my face.

"Natasha Liss?"

I didn't recognize the voice. "Yes?"

"This is Sharon Barkell. You auditioned with us on Wednesday?"

Now I knew her. The choreographer. I slowly stood. "Um...yes?"

"One of our four choices just pulled out thanks to an injury. You were our first choice backup—I would have told you on Wednesday, but you ran out of there before I could—"

"Oh!" I'd frozen, standing in the middle of the dining room with my handbag resting on my bare toes.

"I'll level with you, Natasha. I loved your dancing, but there was just a little too much anger coming through. We need exactly what you gave us, but with a little more lightness and fun. Do you think you could do that?"

A week ago I'd have said no. But now I thought of the man—*my man*—upstairs, the man who loved me despite what he knew, and my heart swelled in my chest. "Yes! Yes, definitely."

I could almost hear her relieved nod. "Okay. Let's do a second audition in a couple of days. Same routine as before but it'll be just you and me. I'll call you with a time—okay?"

"Yes. Absolutely. Totally okay. Thank you!"

I hung up and stared at the phone's screen, wondering if I'd just dreamed the whole thing. The day was getting better and better.

Back in the lobby, I stood at the foot of the staircase and listened. Nothing. I'd managed not to wake him—more good luck.

I cleaned up the spilled coffee. There was just enough left in the packet to brew two mugs, and I carried them upstairs. On the landing, golden sunlight formed what felt like a solid block as it streamed through the window and I stood there in its warmth for a moment, basking. I wasn't sure how to wake him. Subtly—let him smell the coffee? Sexily—kneel over him and let my hair fall in his face? Romantically, with a kiss? Eventually, I decided there was only one way, given the news I'd just had. I'd put the coffee down and jump on the bed, and when he woke up, startled, I'd tell him about the audition.

    I opened the door, and everything went wrong.

CHAPTER TWENTY

Darrell
Four Years Ago

I N SOME TINY, POWERLESS CORNER of my brain, I know that it's a nightmare. That should make it easier, but it doesn't. A nightmare means I can relive it again and again, forever.

We're on week three of my four-week trip to the Middle East. After not seeing my folks since Christmas, being able to spend a full month together feels great, although mom is already driving me crazy with questions on my diet, my love life...even how often I'm doing my laundry. I think partially she's just glad to have me to talk to. We don't see a lot of Dad—he's at the airbase most of the day, watching his new engine go through its paces on the F-35, then doing yet another round of tweaks and fixes. We've managed a handful of family days out, though, exploring the high-end shopping malls and resorts. The area has me a little freaked out, with its complete clash of ancient culture and modern riches. On one level, we're honored guests but on another, we're total outsiders.

We've just picked up Dad in the SUV. It's only four and I figure we can hit the pool in that magic time when the sun's low enough not to frazzle our family's trademark pale skin, but still high enough for us to stretch out and relax. Also, there's a cute blonde staying at the resort who might just be by the poolside....

The SUV pulls up outside the hotel and because it's a nightmare I know what's going to happen. Time seems to slow down. Dad turns around in his seat and finishes up the lame joke he was telling us, and I roll my eyes. Mom pokes him in the ribs and he pokes her back.

I will my muscles to respond, to stay in the car, but I can't change the past. My hand yanks the door lever and the oven-hot desert air rushes in. One leg slides out into the sunshine. I'm in a hurry, wanting to grab my towel and trunks and get down to the pool before Mom and Dad, so I can bag a place close to (but not too close to) the blonde, if she's there.

As I climb out, I see that Dad's hand is on the key. The part of me that's back in the present is screaming *don't turn it, don't turn it*, but however hard I scream, nothing comes out of my mouth. I can't warn him about what'll happen when he switches off the ignition.

Part of me wants him to turn the key right now, before I'm out of the car, but I know he won't. I know he'll listen to the end of this song—another ten seconds.

I slam my door and start to run, but a taxi beeps and I have to stand and wait while it crawls past in front of me. My back is maybe a foot from the SUV. In my mind, I'm counting off the seconds. Four, five, six. Why couldn't it happen now, when we're all still together?

But the taxi moves and I run across the street. Ten

steps that save my life.

I hear a door open behind me and half turn. Mom's just climbing out, smiling about something. That image of her face is burned into my memory forever.

There's a flash of light that makes me scrunch up my face and an instant later an invisible hand picks me up and hurls me into a parked car, the window crunching against my back. White-hot pain erupts in my side, and it doesn't ebb away—it gets worse and worse. I slump down on my ass, my back against a car.

Roiling black smoke hides the SUV for a moment, but then the wind whips it away and I see the blazing, twisted wreck. My parents are gone. I don't understand for a second what's happened, because I can't see Mom and where Dad was sitting there's just—

The burning shape inside the car starts to scream and I try to crawl towards him but every time I move, the pain in my side makes me almost black out.

I listen to him scream for another three minutes before he dies.

CHAPTER TWENTY-ONE

Natasha

HE WAS ASLEEP, but he was talking. Muttering words I couldn't understand, asking—no, *begging* someone. I'd seen people sleep-talk before—Clarissa had been known to do it, when she'd had one too many drinks and crashed out on the couch. But that had been funny, hearing her mumble about some guy she liked and how cute he was. This wasn't funny at all, because I could hear how utterly terrified he was.

As I stepped closer, I could see he was sweating, his chest glistening with it. His limbs were twitching, his eyes darting about under their lids. When I left him, he'd been sleeping peacefully. Whatever this was, it had descended on him fast.

He was shaking his head now, his breath coming in quick, panicked gasps. I put the coffee down and went over to the bed, gingerly reaching out to touch him. "Darrell?"

He didn't hear me. And whatever he was living—or reliving—in his mind, it was reaching some awful peak. His breathing was labored, his face frozen in fear. "Darrell?" I shook him. "Darrell?" Nothing. "Darrell! You're dreaming! Wake up!" I was panicking myself now, my heart racing.

He drew in a long, agonized gasp and then his face contorted into a mask of rage. I took a staggering step back, thinking for a second that he'd woken and was angry with me. But he was still asleep, his head locked in position now, eyes staring behind closed lids at one point in space. I touched his arm and his muscles were steel hard, every tendon straining. It was truly chilling. Whoever was on the receiving end of his wrath, in the dream, would fear for their life. And seeing it happen, seeing the quiet, peaceful man I knew change like this, was almost as frightening for me. Had this been inside him, the whole time?

And then, suddenly, he opened his eyes and stared up at me, panting for air.

"Darrell!" I could tell he wasn't quite seeing me, wasn't sure where he was. I started making shushing noises, trying to calm him, at the same time trying to calm my own fear.

"Darrell, it's *Natasha,*" I told him. He seemed to focus on me, then, and I felt him slide slowly back to reality. The rage left his face and I slumped in relief, collapsing on the bed next to him as I watched him get his breath back.

"Sorry," he told me at last. He wouldn't meet my eyes.

"It's okay." I handed him a cup of coffee, but he just sat staring at it without drinking.

"What did I say?" he asked tightly.

"Nothing that made sense." I slowly put one hand

on his shoulder, and he didn't move it away. "What was it?"

He stared at me for a second, and I thought he was going to tell me. And then he was turning away. "I can't. I'm sorry. I just—I get bad dreams sometimes, you know?"

I did know. I'd had one only that week, while he'd been in Virginia. But my dreams left me shaking with fear. His terrified him at first—and then drove him to an anger so powerful it was frightening. I hugged him close. What had done this to him, burned something so deeply into his mind that it affected him like this even today?

When we moved apart, he finally drank some coffee. "Look. Last night...."

I nodded, glad to get onto something safer.

He looked me right in the eye. "I know I said it before, but I want you to know that I know...and it's okay. I mean, of course it's okay. It doesn't change the way I feel about you. I love you."

Something melted inside me, something that had been trapped in ice for a long, long time. I'd been right. He really did understand. "Thank you," I whispered, feeling hot tears slide down my cheeks. Hope. Hope was back. I'd finally found someone who wouldn't judge me, who wouldn't yell at me, I was in love, I had another shot at my audition...everything was going to work out.

He pulled me into a hug and I felt my tears wet against his shoulder.

"I'm here now, and you're safe," he told me. "He can't hurt you anymore."

I froze. *What?*

I pushed slowly back from the hug, looking at him. The moment stretched out in sickly slow motion. "Who?"

"Your foster dad," he said solemnly.

And all my hopes turned to ash.

"You think—" I couldn't get the words out.

He nodded slowly, thinking I was just denying it. "I know, Natasha. What someone did to you with candles...the scars on your leg. I will never let anyone hurt you. Not ever again."

He thought I'd been abused.

I shook my head. "No." And I said it so suddenly and firmly he shut up. But in the silence that followed, I didn't know what to say. I'd got it completely wrong. He didn't understand at all. He thought he'd discovered some poor, abused girl with an evil father he could get angry at.

"I'm sorry," he said. "If I've got it wrong I'm sorry. It doesn't matter who it was. You're safe now." He kept repeating that: *You're safe now.* As if it was something external I could be saved from. He had no idea.

I shook my head again. "Why are you...why are you trying to *figure this out?*" Suddenly I was blazingly angry. "This is my *private business*—why are you...." I flailed for words but couldn't find them.

He took my face gently between his hands. "Because I love you. I just—I can't bear to think of anyone hurting you."

Any remaining hope died. How angry would he be, when he found out? When he discovered what I did, and why I did it? I stood up and walked to the door. Behind me, I heard him get up.

"Natasha?"

I swallowed. "I need to go."

And I was off and running down the stairs. He ran after me, but I had a head start and was out of the front door before he could catch me.

"Natasha!"

I kept going.

CHAPTER TWENTY-TWO

Natasha

I CALLED A CAB WHEN I got back to the main road and made it to class—just. Luckily, I kept a change of dancing gear in my locker. I really needed to talk to Clarissa, but Tuesday was the one day we didn't have any classes together and I missed her at lunch because I went back to the apartment to have a shower and change.

When I headed home that evening, I had no idea if she was in or out. "Clarissa?" I called as I closed the door of our apartment.

No answer. *Damn.* I really needed to talk to her. I needed to get it all out.

I wandered through to my room and eyed the bike. Escape wasn't what I needed, I decided. I didn't feel like I was sliding out of control. I just felt...tired. Over the years, I'd lost all hope of having a normal life. I'd thought that was bad, but to have hope dangled in front of me, only to discover I'd been wrong...that had crushed me completely.

I threw myself onto my bed. What now? Obviously, things were over with Darrell. If I stayed with him, he was going to keep pushing and pushing, and eventually he'd discover that the monster he was saving me from was me. And then he'd hate me like I hated myself, and I didn't think I could bear that.

Then I heard it. A hard sound I couldn't place. I frowned.

It came again, and this time I identified it. A palm against flesh—someone being slapped. It had come from Clarissa's room. The floor seemed to drop away, ice filling my veins.

A third time, harder than before, and I thought I heard Clarissa sob.

Her door was tightly closed. What should I do? Call 911? Burst in? Who was in there with her—Neil? He was twice my size!

I ran to the kitchen and drew a butcher's knife from the knife rack. I could hear the blood rushing in my ears, my heart pounding as I crept down the corridor towards the door. Another slap. A sob. My fingers tightened around the knife's handle. With the other hand, I turned the doorknob and flung the door wide.

"*Stop!*" I screamed.

....

And then I was back in the hallway. I'd spun back from the doorway and pressed myself up against the wall, the plaster cool against my back. My eyes were squeezed tight shut and what I'd just seen was being vividly replayed in my mind, however much I tried to stop it.

Clarissa, naked, on hands and knees on the bed, her pale ass raised towards Neil as he spanked her. She'd looked over her shoulder at me, horrified, her face as red as mine.

I could hear movement and whispers in her room. I opened my eyes and walked very calmly to the kitchen, put the knife back in the knife block and made coffee.

Clarissa joined me at the table a few minutes later. She managed to come in and sit down without meeting my eyes once.

We sat there in silence for a moment. Clarissa made a gun shape with her hand and mimed shooting herself in the head. Then she let her forehead slump to the table, her hair covering her face.

"It's not that bad," I said at last.

The faceless blonde head nodded. *Yes it is.*

"You did come home and catch me...thinking about Darrell," I told her.

"Everybody does that." She paused. "Well, maybe not in the lounge...."

"See?"

"It's not even in the same league."

I sipped some coffee while I thought, my embarrassment fading a little now that we were actually talking. "It's no big deal. Spanking and bondage and stuff—it's fashionable. Like in that book."

Clarissa finally lifted her head from the table, horrified. "He doesn't *tie me up!*"

"Well, then!"

She hesitated. "I think he wants to, though," she said in a small voice.

"Oh. Well, okay. I mean, as long as you like it."

"I do." She looked away quickly, flushing. "I just don't get what he *does* to me. It's like he flips a switch in my brain and suddenly I'm all.... He's so *totally* not my type, but he just...." She gave a groan of frustration.

I sipped my coffee and smirked. "Like in the kitchen at Darrell's house."

Her jaw dropped. "You *saw?*" She thumped the table with her fist. "I *thought* you saw, but you didn't say anything!"

"I think he's cute. I think you're cute together."

She shuddered. "Eww. Don't. I don't want to be cute. And I don't know if I want to be some guy's...*plaything*." She finally picked up her coffee and started to drink. After a moment, she said, "And the irony is, *you're* the one dating the billionaire."

Then she saw the look on my face, and her smile collapsed.

Neil came in and kissed Clarissa on the back of the head, completely unembarrassed. We sat in silence as he made himself a sandwich. When he tried to coax her back to bed, she waved him away.

"Okay," she said as soon as he'd gone back to the bedroom. "What's wrong?"

"We had sex," I said at last.

She waited.

"Then we had a fight."

She nodded.

"He found the scars."

Clarissa bit her lip. She'd known I cut myself for about a year. I'd been standing on a chair to put the waffle maker back on top of the kitchen cupboard, had slipped off the chair and wound up on the floor with my skirt up around my waist. Like Darrell, she'd assumed the cuts were the work of someone else, and I'd had to tell her the truth before she called the cops on my recent ex-boyfriend. The following month had been hell. She'd been angry at me, angry at herself, hurt I hadn't told her before...all the things I didn't want Darrell to go through.

She'd finally accepted that it wasn't a problem she could fix, though, and that I wasn't going to tell her the reason I did it. After another few months, we'd returned to something approaching normalcy. I knew it still bothered her but, as long as I kept myself out of the emergency room, she accepted it. It became an unpleasant little habit we didn't discuss.

I knew that with Darrell, it wouldn't be the same. I'd grown to understand his mind and could see the way he observed and recorded and fixed things. I knew he'd want to fix me. Cutting myself would go completely against his logical view of the world, and he wouldn't stop until he understood *why*. Once we got to that point, we were lost. He'd either hate me because I wouldn't tell him, or hate me when he found out the truth.

"How'd he take it?" I could feel Clarissa watching me steadily as I stared at the chips on my Knicks mug.

"He thought someone else did them." I refused to look at her, but it didn't matter. I could *see* her in my mind, pressing her lips disapprovingly together. "I ran."

"You really like him." Not a question.

I didn't answer.

"Maybe he'd be a good person to talk about it with." *Since you won't tell me,* she might as well have added.

I shook my head.

"Nat—"

"I can't." I got up and walked out.

And then I went to my room and got on the bike.

Helena Newbury

CHAPTER TWENTY-THREE

Darrell
Ten minutes earlier

MEETING NATASHA HAD changed everything. I'd had the nightmare a hundred times before and my solution to the rage had always been the same. Go to the workshop and *work,* create something that would hurt the people who'd taken my parents from me. It didn't make the anger go away, but it focused it...directed it outward so that it didn't destroy me. But today....

Today, when I'd woken from the nightmare the first thing I'd seen was her terrified face. I'd scared the hell out of her. And then I'd made it worse by pushing and pushing to know about her past. When she'd left, I'd had no idea what to do and had wound up in the workshop, hammering and welding. My normal solution—only it no longer did any good. However many times I heard that glorious, metallic ringing, it didn't ease the anger inside me or the guilt over how I'd hurt

Natasha.

This wasn't something that was going to get better with time. I needed to *do* something. Three times I picked up the phone to call her, but I had no idea what to say. By the evening, I was going out of my mind. I knew when I was out of my depth. I called Neil.

"Uh huh?"

I frowned. "You're breathing heavy. Are you at the gym?"

"No. Clarissa's place."

I heard the creak of a bed. "Should I call back? The two of you aren't—"

"We were. Natasha and her just left."

"*What?*"

"Chill, you idiot. Natasha walked in on us. Clarissa's gone to the kitchen to explain."

"Explain?"

"There was spanking."

I sighed. Neil never did things by halves. "How did she look?"

"Fantastic. Smokin' hot bod. We started out up against the wall—"

"*Natasha!* How did Natasha look? Did she look upset?"

"I didn't get a good look at her." He paused, his tone suddenly serious. "Why?"

I sighed. "We had a fight."

"*Oh.* You want me to go see?"

"Yeah."

"Hold up. I'll go make a sandwich."

I heard him put the phone down and then had to go quietly crazy for five minutes while he took his time in the kitchen. I strained my ears, but I could only hear a faint whisper of voices.

I didn't understand her reaction. Someone had

clearly hurt her—cut her or scratched her or something, on her thigh, and harmed her in some way with candles. Who, if not her foster dad? My gut tightened as I thought of someone, anyone, hurting her.

By the time Neil picked up the phone, I was going crazy. "How did she look?

"There's definitely something wrong with her, man. They shut up when I came in. What did you do to her?"

I couldn't tell him the details. "Nothing." I sighed. "Something. I'm not sure."

"You're crazy, man. First girl you really like in years and you *fight* with her?"

"I've dated other girls."

"But you haven't *liked* them."

And he was right. They'd been rich and pretty and utterly vacuous. Natasha was different.

"Okay, I'm an idiot," I told Neil.

"I already knew that. What'd you fight about?"

"Just some stuff in her past. I wanted to know, and she didn't want to tell me."

"Oh." Neil sounded like he suddenly understood. "You mean: she had a secret and you were being you."

"What does that mean?"

"Obsessive and a pain in the ass."

I gaped. "I'm not obsessive. I'm...thorough."

"Which is awesome when you're working but not good with fragile chicks."

I thought about that. "I didn't know she was fragile. Natasha's fragile?"

"Everybody's fragile, man."

"Even you?"

"Maybe not me. Everybody else."

I sighed. "Okay, okay. Stay out of her past. What else?"

"Call her."

CHAPTER TWENTY-FOUR

Natasha

I HAD MY HEAD DOWN, ASS UP, legs pumping hard on the pedals. I'd only been going for a few minutes, but I had the bike cranked up to maximum resistance and my muscles were already starting to protest. I hadn't warmed up and was at real risk of tearing something, but I didn't care.

Stupid, I told myself. *Stupid, stupid, stupid.* Thinking it could work. Thinking I could have a relationship. All I'd done was taunt myself—let myself have a taste of everything I'd been missing, making its loss all the more bitter. I'd let him get too close, let my attraction for him make me forget what I really was. And then, just as I deserved, it had all come tumbling down.

I pedaled harder, panting now. The whir of the bike rose and rose. I'd ride until my legs burned. Until I damn well *did* tear something, serve me right for—

My phone rang.

I knew it was him, but I grabbed it and checked

the screen anyway.

I kept pedaling, staring at the phone as it rang and rang. I'd just keep going. He'd get the message eventually. Probably count himself lucky that he'd escaped without getting too deeply involved.

I was going faster and faster, my chest heaving, the air like lava. The phone kept ringing and ringing, about to go to voicemail. I gritted my teeth, waiting for it to ring off—

And then, without consciously doing it, I'd hit "Answer" and my legs stopped moving. I couldn't speak for a second, I was so out of breath, so we both sat there listening to my labored panting.

"Natasha?" he said at last.

I didn't answer. I had no idea what to say. I heard the bike's flywheel slowly spinning down.

"Natasha?" he sounded worried, now. I could hear my heart thumping, and it wasn't slowing down like it should.

"Nat—"

"What?" My voice didn't sound like my own. It sounded angry and afraid, like a wounded animal ready to lash out.

"I'm sorry."

It almost made me angrier. Why did he have to be nice? This would be so much easier if I could be mad at him. But that was the worst part—I knew his intentions were good.

"I don't think...." My eyes stung, and I told myself it was just sweat trickling into them. "I don't think we should see each other again."

"No!" So loud and forceful I jumped. "Natasha, no! I'm sorry. I'm sorry I pried. I just—I want to protect you."

My eyes were getting hotter and hotter. I wiped

them savagely with the back of my hand and it came away wet. He didn't get it. He wanted to know who'd hurt me so he could be mad at them. When he discovered I was hurting myself, he'd be mad at *me*. And then, inevitably, he'd want to know why I did it, and if I told him *that* he'd hate me forever.

Better to end it now.

I realized I'd been silent for too long. "I don't think it's going to work out, Darrell." I thought of losing him, of never looking into those deep, clear eyes again. Of never feeling the push of his pecs against my chest, smooth and warm and so solidly *real*. I could feel myself slipping away again, and now that I'd started to get used to my new anchor, I wasn't sure the old one would work anymore. I could feel the hot tears rolling down my cheeks.

"Natasha...." I could hear that he was choosing every word very carefully. And somehow I knew that this was as new to him as it was to me, that he wasn't used to this sort of conversation. The fact he was trying made my heart melt. "I love you. I promise I will never, ever, ask about your past again. OK? It's off limits."

I felt a little flicker of hope inside me and immediately tried to stamp down on it, because I knew I was kidding myself. This was Darrell, with his brilliant mind and his eyes that saw everything. There was no way he was going to leave it alone. Not forever. A week from now or a year from now, he'd need to know, and breaking it off then would hurt even more.

But...ending it now, when there was even the faint possibility of us being happy together...wasn't that worse?

I could hear him at the other end of the line, listening. He could tell I was thinking. Maybe he could even tell I was crying. I could feel him bursting to speak, desperate to say the magic words that would fix everything, but not knowing what they were.

There weren't any. I knew I couldn't be fixed. I didn't deserve to be fixed. And if I wanted to be happy, I had to be the one to make the leap. I had to decide if it was worth lying to him—every single day—and always having that distance between us, if it meant we could be happy.

"Okay," I said, in a voice I could barely hear.

I heard him let out a long sigh of relief. We were both still edgy and nervous. The bridge we'd gradually built between us had been swept away, and all we had now was a slender rope that could snap at any time.

"Will you come to the party tomorrow?" He was reaching out into space. The party would be full of intimidating posh, rich people and as his date, I'd be the center of attention....

But I'd be with him.

I felt for that strong, warm mental hand and grasped it. "Yes," I told him. "But I have to go now." And I hung up, because I knew if I said even one more word I was going to break down completely. I looked down at the bike, but that wasn't what I needed. I climbed off, legs aching and cramped, and collapsed on my bed. I didn't want to cut, or pedal, or cry. I just lay there, staring numbly up at the peeling paint on the ceiling, and let it all sink in. *What the hell,* I asked myself, *is going to happen now?*

CHAPTER TWENTY-FIVE

Darrell

I WAS SITTING DOWN IN THE WORKSHOP— completely inappropriate, given that I was in a suit for the party, but upstairs, the caterers were bustling around with trays of canapés and glasses and in the garden the string quartet were tuning up. The workshop was the only place I could think. Normally, I'd have had the music cranked up loud to drown out my thoughts and memories, but I needed silence, needed to work through everything that had been happening. What struck me immediately was how weird it felt. I was starting to realize that I'd been cramming my mind full of work ever since my parents died, unwilling to stop for even one second.

Natasha was affecting me, right down to my very core. It was more than the way she moved, it was—okay, I know it sounds stupid, but it was her *spirit*. She was all gentleness and grace; I'd always been about brute force and speed. Maybe it was time I stopped. Maybe going at full speed had taken me somewhere I didn't want to be.

I couldn't think of the day it happened—it was too painful. But I could think of the days and months after. The police, and the American embassy, explaining that my parents had been targeted because of their involvement with the military. That the most likely suspects were anti-American extremists who'd chosen a soft target in the rich Arab state we'd been visiting instead of engaging troops in Iraq or Afghanistan. That they lived in the mountains, and that they'd taken to sheltering in fortified caves that could withstand an initial missile strike, allowing them to escape before the next one.

I'd returned to the US and buried my parents. I'd expected the anger to decrease, but it only built. Days after the funeral, the same terrorists had attacked the airbase itself, and then an international school.

A week later, I'd returned to MIT and looked at the blueprint on my dorm room wall. I'd been working on a cheap, long-distance aircraft intended to bring disaster relief to remote areas of the world.

I'd grabbed the center of the blueprint and ripped it from the wall. And then I'd sat down at my computer and started designing something that would smash down into the cowards' caves like the fist of God himself.

A month later, I'd taken my design to five different aerospace companies, and none of them had wanted anything to do with a messed-up college kid who looked like he hadn't slept in a week. And then a young research and development exec at Sabre had taken a look, and had flown all the way from Virginia to come and talk to me.

I can help you, Carol had told me. *We need people like you, people who understand what it takes to win a war.* She was so calming and loving, after months spent on my own. She'd told me, *These people took your parents. Don't ever forget that.* And I never did.

Sometimes, I'd come up with ideas myself. More often, Carol told me about some problem Sabre were having, to nudge me in the right direction.

I hadn't really admitted it to myself until that moment, but over the years, their requests had moved further and further away from things used to fight terrorists. I walked over to the prototype missile and ran my hand down its casing. It wasn't designed to kill a handful of extremists hiding in a cave. It was designed to destroy a city, and its parent weapon, a country.

I sat down heavily. What had I become?

Helena Newbury

CHAPTER TWENTY-SIX

Natasha

W E COULD SEE GRAY STORM CLOUDS spreading just a few miles away, but the sky immediately overhead was postcard blue and the three of us soaked up the sunshine as we waited on the doorstep. Clarissa, looking like she belonged there, in a light, floaty dress that would have been at home at a polo match. Neil, who'd eventually let Clarissa persuade him to put on a shirt and a slightly less ragged pair of jeans. And me, in a dress borrowed from Clarissa, feeling completely out of place. It wasn't as if I went to many parties, but a party in the middle of the afternoon, in a sundress?

We could hear classical music trickling in from the gardens behind the house, and when Darrell opened the door there was a waiter beside him offering us chilled champagne. I let Clarissa and Neil sweep in ahead of me and stood on the step with Darrell.

"Hi." I didn't know what else to say. The phone

call suddenly seemed unreal, as if we needed to make up all over again in person, and I had no idea how to do that. I looked into those achingly clear blue eyes and I could see the pain he was in. He stepped in close, his hands coming to rest on my cheeks, and I had to tilt my head back to look up at him.

"I will never ask about your past again," he told me solemnly, and pulled me into his chest. I rested my cheek against the solid wall of him, my arms around his waist, and slowly relaxed into him. All my doubts since the call gradually melted away.

When I finally pulled back, he gave me a glass of champagne and led me into the house by the hand, squeezing it gently. I squeezed back.

I hadn't seen much of the gardens until now. They stretched out behind the mansion for a good half acre, with manicured lawns and winding, tree-lined paths—a good place to lose yourself for an hour or so. I tried to imagine Darrell walking in them and couldn't. I suspected that, like the rest of the house, he saw them as just a freebie that came with the workshop.

A string quartet was playing under a sun shade and waiters circulated with chilled drinks and canapés. For the next two hours, I smiled and shook hands and occasionally kissed cheeks as Darrell introduced me to local dignitaries. I got the impression they weren't so much friends as people he was expected to mix with. The conversation seemed to be a mixture of which charities people were donating too, which gallery opening they were attending and which ski resort they were vacationing at. I felt, just as I thought I would, completely out of place.

But his arm around my waist was all I needed to make it bearable. With it there, all the questions about dancing and Fenbrook and where I was from seemed polite, not threatening—why was it so hard when I was on my own? I rarely felt like I was in danger of panicking and sliding out of control, and on the rare occasion when someone asked something about my past and I felt myself start to go, I only had to press myself against the solidity of his arm and I was calm again. After a while, I even started to enjoy myself. I caught a few vicious little glances from a couple of ridiculously skinny girls when they saw me with Darrell. Exes? Or just hoping to try their luck? I nestled closer to Darrell. *Tough. He's mine and I'm keeping him!*

As the party wound down, the storm clouds were almost overhead and everyone kept commenting on how lucky we'd been. Clarissa and Neil had spent most of the party bickering good-naturedly, with an occasional whisper from Neil making Clarissa suddenly gasp and blush. We both shook our heads as we looked at them.

"I can't believe Clarissa's found someone who can reduce her to silence," I said.

"I can't believe Neil's found someone who can persuade him to put a shirt on," Darrell told me.

The party was at an end and people were drifting off when we heard the voice behind us. "Well." The accent was British and deceptively warm, with a layer of pure ice beneath it. "I'm guessing this must be Natasha."

I turned. She was maybe ten years' older than me, with long dark hair, and looked if anything more stylish than Clarissa in her sundress. Unlike me, she looked like she regularly went to garden parties—with the Queen.

"Natasha, this is Carol. She works for Sabre Technologies—they buy the stuff I make."

Carol smiled at me. "Darrell's our little star. We've been together for four years now." She deliberately made it sound ambiguous and then made it worse by leaning over and kissing his cheek. "I'm really quite protective of him."

I smiled sweetly while resisting the urge to rip her throat out. "You must know him very well, after four years." Had he slept with her? She was a lot older than me, but very attractive....

"Oh, I know all his little foibles. I'm so glad he found himself a...." Her eyes flicked down my body. "*Muse.*" She somehow made it sound like "slut."

Darrell took her by the elbow and steered her away. "I actually need to speak to Carol downstairs for a moment," he told me. "Will you be okay?"

I wasn't overjoyed at being left on my own, especially if it was so that he could talk shop, but I smiled. "Of course."

I watched them walk into the elevator together. Darrell didn't act like there was anything between them—not sexually, at least—but she sure did. And Darrell had been antsy as soon as she showed up, his face tight with worry. What was going on—and why wasn't he telling me about it?

The house was emptying now, the string quartet putting away their instruments. I tried to find Clarissa, but couldn't. I gave up and went to stand in the hallway, where I'd be more likely to see her when she came past. I leaned back against the staircase. A few moments later, something pushed against my back, and when I stepped forward, a door opened behind me.

Neil emerged from the storage closet, closing the door behind him. I looked at him, bemused. "What were you doing in there?"

The door opened again and Clarissa's head popped out, looking both ways to see if the coast was clear and then blushing as she saw me. She slunk out, still in the process of tugging her dress down.

"You two are unbelievable," I muttered. "At least

sneak upstairs and use a bedroom!"

Clarissa sniffed. "It's a billionaire's house. I thought there might be a dungeon or something under there."

"*Millionaire* and he doesn't—oh, forget it."

"Are you coming back into the city with us?" she asked.

I hadn't thought about that. After the fight and our make-up phone call, we'd only made the vaguest of plans. A night of just the two of us was exactly what we needed. "I'll stay here."

Unexpectedly, she gave me a squeeze. "Be careful." And then she was gone, towing Neil with her.

I wandered the house as the last few guests drifted out, and then it was just the caterers and me. There was no sign of Carol or Darrell, and my stomach started to churn. It wasn't that I thought they were doing anything, just...something about the woman put me on edge.

I rounded a corner and suddenly she was there in front of me, knocking back a glass of champagne, another one ready in her other hand. When she saw me, her eyes narrowed and she stalked over. "What bollocks have you been whispering in his ear?" she demanded.

"What?"

"Don't *what* me: you know exactly what I'm talking about. Did you tell him you'd only spread your legs if he went peacenik? Did that bloody hippy have a hand in it, too?"

I had no idea what she was talking about, but the part about spreading my legs made me want to slap her across the face. "Maybe you'd better leave."

"Oh, it's *your* house now, is it? Think you've snagged yourself a millionaire?" She got right up in my face. "Wait until your novelty wears off, sweetie. I've known him a lot longer than you and he'll choose the work over the sex every time, and I don't care how pretty your pirouettes are!"

She deliberately dropped her glass and let it shatter on the tiles. Then she was stalking out of the front door, staggering just a little in her heels. A moment later I heard a sports car's engine roar into life and she sped off, far too drunk to be driving. *With any luck, she'll get pulled over,* I thought viciously.

What the hell had she been talking about? *Peacenik?!*

I needed answers. I took the elevator down to the workshop.

CHAPTER TWENTY-SEVEN

Darrell

I WAS SITTING ON THE FLOOR, my back against a workbench. The fight with Carol had exhausted me.

When I'd told her I was starting to have doubts about my work, she'd actually thought I was joking—the champagne she'd knocked back hadn't helped. It wasn't until she took a good look at my expression that she'd sobered up.

"You have *doubts?!*" she'd said, disbelievingly. "When have you ever had doubts? *You* came to *me,* remember? You were the one who wanted into this game!"

"It isn't a game," I'd told her tightly. "And it isn't the same anymore."

I'd meant since the weapons had grown bigger, since we'd started measuring success in thousands of deaths, in city blocks destroyed. But I'd seen her eyes flick up towards the mansion. Towards Natasha. She presumed Natasha knew, of course. I didn't correct her. I figured that if she thought she already knew, there was less chance she'd tell her out of spite.

She'd asked me if I'd wanted more money, or an in-house workshop at the company, or an assistant. I'd shook my head and told her I wasn't sure why I was doing it anymore.

At which point she walked to the back of the lab and tore down my Curious Weasels poster. She'd known what was behind it, of course. I'd only put the poster up to cover it minutes before Natasha arrived to dance for the first time. I'd been planning to take it back down each time she left, but weirdly, I'd found myself leaving it in place.

Behind the poster was a photo. A black and white crime scene photo of the SUV, twisted and blackened, firefighting foam still dripping from it. I'd asked, then pleaded, then demanded a copy and the lead investigator had eventually relented. It had been the image that had kept me going through the all-nighters, kept me pushing at the problems when they resisted every attempt at a solution. I had only to look at the photo and I'd know that I had to keep going.

Carol had plucked it from the wall and held it in front of my face, following me with it when I tried to turn away. "Have you forgotten?" she asked me. "Do you not remember *who this is?*"

And the memories had risen up inside me like a dark wave and I'd slumped to the floor. She'd crouched down in front of me and talked to me as if I was a child. Telling me how it was natural for me to be exhausted, towards the end of a long project. How I should maybe take a break—a full week or even two—before the next one.

"You're a hero," she'd told me. "A bloody American hero, even if you don't get any of the limelight.

It was people like you who won the Second World War, the scientists and inventors toiling away behind the scenes."

We're not at war, I'd tried to say. But my mind was full of hot desert air and the blare of the taxi as it sped past me. I'd nodded, reluctantly, and she'd stood up and left, dropping the photo at my feet. She wasn't happy, but she knew I was back on board—for now, at least.

I sighed and knocked my head gently against the workbench. Maybe I could stop, after this project. Finish the missile and then tell Carol it was over. Natasha never had to know. I'd managed to keep it from her so far. Another few weeks....

I heard the elevator doors open and watched Natasha walk straight past me. The room was in half-darkness—I'd only bothered to switch on a few of the lights when I came down with Carol—and the workbench blocked me from sight. She walked right up to the missile, staring at the sheet that covered it. Jesus, had Carol told her? But she didn't look angry...just confused. I watched as she tentatively reached a hand towards the sheet, and there was a part of me that wanted her to find out. I was so sick of lies, and I wanted so badly to talk to her about what was going on. Maybe, if I stopped work on the missile right now, just shipped it off to Carol half-finished and washed my hands of it, Natasha could forgive me....

Except I couldn't do that. I'd poured my soul into the project. I couldn't stop it now any more than I could stop caring for a child. I wasn't even sure I was going to be able to walk away from my work when the project was done, and I knew that was Carol's plan: let me finish one and then hook me with the next.

Natasha's hand touched the sheet and I stood up.

"Hi."

"Jesus!" she spun, dropping her handbag in the process, and things went skittering across the floor.

"Sorry." I stretched and walked over to her, pulling her into a hug.

She wound her arms around me. "Is everything okay?"

I gazed over her shoulder at the sheet-covered missile. "Carol and I had a disagreement. Work stuff."

"Yeah, I figured. I ran into her upstairs."

I moved her gently back, so I could look at her. "Oh?"

She shook her head. "She was drunk. Seemed to think I was a bad influence on you."

I relaxed a little and kissed the top of her head. "I like your influence." I really meant it. Being torn between her and my work was bad...but being oblivious to what I was doing, having my work and nothing else? I couldn't even imagine going back to that now. Somehow, I had to figure out a way to have both, to keep Natasha *and* do right by my parents.

"You missed the end of the party," she told me. "Everyone's gone. Do you want to come upstairs? Maybe sit in the garden? There's plenty of champagne left and it hasn't started raining—yet."

Actually, sitting out in the garden with her, watching the sun go down with a bottle of champagne sounded like exactly what I needed. I hugged her close again. "You go ahead. I'll be up in exactly one minute. I just have one thing I need to do."

I swept the stuff that had spilled out of her handbag back into it and gave it back to her, then watched her go up in the elevator. Only then did I walk over to the workbench where I'd been sitting and retrieve the photo of the SUV. I wasn't sure I wanted it up on the wall again, even underneath the poster, but I couldn't bring myself to throw it away, either. Eventually, I settled for putting it away at the bottom of a drawer. When I closed it, I felt somehow...lighter. I wondered if I'd reached a turning point.

I was heading for the elevator when I saw something glinting under a table.

CHAPTER TWENTY-EIGHT

Natasha

UPSTAIRS, THE CATERERS HAD LEFT and the house and gardens were quiet. The sky was fully gray now, and a breeze was getting up. There was still enough warmth left in the air that it was pleasant, though, and as long as the rain held off for a few minutes, we could still enjoy the sunset. I picked up a half-full bottle of champagne and two glasses and wandered out into the garden. I pushed the door shut behind me, realizing too late that it only opened from the inside. I'd have to go around to the front and ring the bell to get back in. I'd have to hope Darrell joined me soon, or I'd be caught outside in the rain.

Picking a spot where Darrell would see me when he came out but where some trees would shelter us from the breeze, I sat down on the grass and tucked my legs under me. With Carol gone and just the two of us alone, this could be a magical evening. We'd watch the sunset together, then maybe go out somewhere for dinner...and

197

finally, that big, four-poster bed. I smiled.

I wondered what exactly they'd fought about. Had Carol tried to rekindle some past relationship, or was that just my paranoia at work? If she had, Darrell had obviously turned her down. Had she wanted him to work even harder, and he'd told her he was putting me first? That would certainly explain her outburst, though I was still bemused by the talk of peaceniks and hippies.

What made me happiest was what Darrell had said when I'd arrived at the house. The past was off limits, and maybe, *maybe*, if we could keep it locked away there, we had a shot at a normal relationship. I hadn't even cut in days....

I froze. Whenever I thought about the past, about cutting, I always touched the cigarette case. It was an unconscious thing, like a child stroking their security blanket. Except my fingers suddenly couldn't find it.

I pulled open my bag and rooted through it. Then, with growing panic, I tipped it upside down and emptied out the contents, rifling through them on the ground. Nothing.

It must have spilled out of my bag, down in the workshop.

Darrell was in the workshop.

I ran for the house.

CHAPTER TWENTY-NINE

Darrell

I PICKED UP THE THING and examined it—it definitely wasn't something of mine. Then I remembered Natasha dropping her handbag, and her things spilling out.

It was like a woman's powder compact, only bigger and rectangular, and I vaguely remembered seeing something like it in an old movie. A cigarette case.

I turned it over and over in my hands. I knew she didn't smoke. I was certain I would have smelt it on her. What, then?

Obviously, I shouldn't open it. It was something personal. I moved towards the elevator again. I'd give it back to her unopened.

At that moment, the doorbell rang. On the security monitor, I could see Natasha knocking at the front door. Worried. Scared, even.

I looked down at the case. What if it was something about her past? A photo, maybe, like the one I kept of the SUV. The person who'd abused her?

The doorbell rang again. Then again. She was frantic.

What if I looked and didn't tell her? What if I could get a hint of what had happened to her? I could tell her I hadn't looked, but I'd be better prepared to help her. At least I'd know what *not* to say. I was desperate to help her—I had to take any opportunity I could.

I fingered the case. I knew that whoever had abused her, it wouldn't stop me loving her. I'd never tell her I knew.

I pressed the button, and the top sprang open.

CHAPTER THIRTY

Natasha

I KNOCKED, THEN BANGED, then hammered on the door, the noise almost lost in a rumble of thunder from above. My panic had turned into a cold, gnawing dread in my gut. Why would he take so long to answer? Unless....

He opened the door and I knew immediately that he'd looked inside the case. He didn't have it in his hands, but I recognized his expression. I'd seen the same thing when Clarissa found out.

I never thought I'd have to see that expression on him.

I took a step backwards. "You opened it," I whispered.

He was staring at me with something between raw anger and pity. "How could you do it?" he asked in a halting voice. "Why would you hurt yourself?" And just like Clarissa, he wasn't asking for an actual reason. What he meant was, *Nothing could possibly be so bad that a sane person would do that.* Except it *was* that bad. He'd never understand.

"Why did you open it?" I took another half step back.

He took one step forwards, on the doorstep now, shaking his head. "Why would you—" He stretched his hands out towards me. "Natasha, you're so beautiful. Why would you hurt yourself?"

I'm not beautiful. Not on the inside. You don't know what I've done. I had to keep backing away, stay out of reach of him, so I could run. I could feel the whole world sliding away from me, ready to send me tumbling six years back through time.

We stood there staring at each other. It was worse—much worse—than it had been when Clarissa found out. She'd been a friend; Darrell was a part of me. I felt as if I was bleeding—he'd ripped something away and exposed my blackened, ugly core, the part I never wanted him to see. I wanted to scream and rage at him for destroying what we'd had together, for blowing my one chance at happiness, but I knew he wouldn't understand.

So I turned and walked away, scrunching down the gravel driveway towards the road, a breadcrumb trail of tears behind me.

"Natasha, please!"

I heard his footsteps behind me and walked faster, barely able to see, now.

"Wait! We have to—"

I broke into run, but then his hand was on my elbow, spinning me around, his face right up close to mine.

"Natasha, you have to let me help you! I can't let you keep on doing this!"

And finally, I cracked.

"*Why?*" I screamed at him. "Why? Why can't you let me? I've been doing this for years and managing *just fine!* Why do you—Jesus, why do you think you have to *fix* me?!"

He took a step back, stunned at my rage. "But you're hurting yourself." *As if I didn't know that.* "I love you. I can't let you hurt yourself."

You love what you think I am. "It's not your right!" I was hysterical now, tears streaming down my face, crying so hard I thought I was going to throw up. "You don't get to decide what I do with—It's *my* body! *Mine!*"

He shook his head. I almost understood. He wanted to protect me from myself; he didn't realize he was getting between me and the one thing that let me cope. And I could see him starting to lose it. "I just don't—*why?* Why would you willingly hurt yourself? It makes no sense!"

I put my hands to my head. "It's not—It's not like I *want* to do it."

"Then stop!"

"It's not that easy! You don't understand...."

He took a deep breath. "Natasha, I love you. I love you for who you are...."

You don't know who I am. You don't know the real me.

He continued, "...you don't need to do something like this to get me to...focus on you."

I think my jaw actually dropped open at that. "You think I'm doing this for *attention?*"

He flushed, and I knew that was exactly what he'd been thinking.

"Do you think that's what I'm like—like a kid holding his breath until his parents give in?" It was difficult to speak, my face crumpled and red now from crying.

He was getting angry now—just as Clarissa had done when she'd found out. "Then tell me! Stop telling me what it isn't and tell me why you do it!"

"I can't!"

"Why not?"

Because you'll hate me. The way he kept pushing and pushing for an answer finally tipped me over the edge. "*I had it under control!*" I screamed at him. "I had it under control—I haven't even cut since Tuesday! It was all fine, it was better since I met you and now...." I trailed off. *Now it's all ruined.*

The clouds finally let go, three or four warning drops and then the deluge began. It was the sort of rain that hissed and chilled, like solid lances of water stabbing straight down into us. We were soaked in seconds, but we just stood there glaring at each other.

I could see it dawn on him. He'd thought he was saving me. He was just realizing that he'd stepped between an addict and their needle, a child and their security blanket. He grabbed my shoulders, his eyes panicked. "Natasha, *please*. Come back inside the house. We can talk about it."

I shook myself free and stepped back. My dress was stuck to me like a second skin, my bare calves running with water. Everything we'd built together was ruined, and that made me so horribly, sickly angry that I shook. It wasn't the pure, cleansing rage I'd felt before. It was old anger that was bitter and bloated and rotten from having been bottled up for so long, since the revelation that night when I was fifteen: *I'm never going to be a normal person now.* I'd escaped, with Darrell— for a wonderful handful of days, I'd stepped outside my fate and lived another life. And now I was being plunged back into it and that made my very soul howl in pain. I took another step back.

"Let me help," he said desperately. "Let me help you." He reached for me, just our fingertips touching.

I turned and walked, heels sinking into the soaked gravel of the drive.

He ran alongside me, spluttering with the water coursing down his face, trying to blink it away. "Natasha, you'll get pneumonia. It's a mile back to the road. Come inside, we can talk!"

I could feel myself closing down, everything drawing into a tight knot at the center of my body, the rest of me cold and dead. I shook my head, a tight little movement, and kept walking.

I heard him stop and drop away behind me. Then he said, desperately, "Don't give up on us!"

I stopped. Is that what he thought—that *I* was giving up on us? I wanted him, more than I'd ever wanted anything in the world. But I knew where this was headed. He'd want to—*need* to—fix me, and he'd keep pushing for an answer. When I refused, he'd get angry again. Or he'd eventually wear me down and I'd tell him, and then he'd swing from love to hate.

But what if I was wrong? What if I was throwing this away based on everyone else I'd met, not based on him? What if he was different?

Every inch of my body was urging me on, pulling me towards the road. He'd stopped following me, leaving it as my decision. I could walk off, get a cab, and never see him again. My secret would be safe and I could go back to my old life.

Only...I didn't want my old life anymore.

I turned to him. The rain made it impossible to see tears, but I could see how red his eyes were. I could feel my soaked dress draining every last ounce of heat from my body, and I hugged myself with my arms. Behind him, the mansion—warmth and shelter. But I couldn't imagine being shut inside it with him, in the quiet of the workshop or the stately elegance of the dining room. I needed neutral ground, so I could run if I had to. "Out here," I told him. "We talk out here." It was important to me, somehow, that he accepted that condition. Maybe I had to feel like I had some control over things, or maybe I just wanted to know he cared about my feelings, after he'd so viciously invaded my privacy.

His face lit up at the faint possibility of hope. He looked around. "But it's—" He saw the look in my eyes, the way I was just barely holding it together. "Okay! Okay, out here." He reached for my hand. "Come on."

I looked at his hand warily, as if it might bite. "I'm not going inside."

"We're not going inside. Come on."

I took a deep breath and took his hand. I'd give it one last try.

***

As we got closer and closer to the mansion, I started to hang back, stretching our joined hands to breaking point. But we didn't go to the door. We went around to the side, and then into the garden, where I'd waited for him happily on the grass. The bottle and glasses I'd brought out were still there, half full of cold rainwater. By now, I was shaking with cold, my arms and legs numb with it.

He led me around a corner, to an area the party hadn't reached. There was dark timber decking, with beams holding up a pointed roof—a mini-bandstand, almost. And in the center of the decking, a squat timber box as high as my hip, covered with a padded blue lid.

Darrell pushed off the lid and steam rose up in a cloud.

"A hot tub?" I said disbelievingly. "You want to get in a hot tub...*now?*"

He indicated the crashing rain outside. "It's out of the rain—but still outside." He shivered, and he wasn't acting. "And doesn't a hot tub sound like a really good idea right now?"

It was utterly insane. We were in the middle of a blazing row, on the verge of breaking up. But I was *freezing.*

"We can just talk," he told me. "Until the rain stops."

I looked at the tub, at the snakes of steam drifting upwards from it. I was trying to stop my teeth from chattering—the water looked incredibly inviting.

"I'm not taking my clothes off," I told him. I couldn't bear the idea of him staring at my scars.

He blinked at me, and then pulled off his shoes and jacket and climbed into the tub in his shirt and pants. The groan of ecstasy as his body hit the steaming water didn't sound fake. He sat down, the water rising to his shoulders, and looked up at me.

Decision time. Did I dare risk another talk with him? I was in enough pain already—why would I open myself up to more?

I looked into his eyes as he sat there, that pure crystal blue that let me see right into his very soul.

I kicked off my heels and stepped into the tub, gasping as the steaming water unfroze my bare legs. My dress stopped clinging to my skin and unfurled in the water, billowing around me. I sunk down until only my shoulders were out, and then sat on the seat opposite him. We both sat in silence for a moment, letting the heat soak into our chilled bodies.

"I'm sorry I yelled at you," I said at last.

"I'm sorry I pushed." Under the deep, bass rumble of his voice, I could hear the fear. He knew he'd come within a hair's breadth of losing me. We were still balanced on the edge of the precipice, stable only because we'd stopped moving. Somehow, we had to claw our way back to safety, and I knew it was going to have to be me who did most of the talking. When he'd tried to guess at the reasons, that had just annoyed me more. I had to explain it to him.

I took a deep breath and looked straight into his eyes, and that seemed to calm me.

"It's not for attention. It's not to hurt myself. I mean, it *is* hurting myself, but that's not why I do it." I stopped and thought, and marveled at his self-control. I knew he had a million questions, but he was letting me do it at my own pace. "It's not about pain—it doesn't even hurt much. It's not about damaging myself." I took another deep, shuddering breath. "It's...about control, I guess. Having something real that I can hang onto. Something stable and solid that will always be there."

I stopped for a second because I could see the question in his eyes. "Yes. You're like that: you're solid and real. That's why I'd stopped doing it, but—" My throat tightened up. "I don't want you to think that—that you have to"—I sniffed—"I don't want to put that on you and make you feel like—"

He reached out and brushed some of the sodden tangles of hair off my face, making the little *shh*ing noises. "I will always be there," he told me.

I sniffed and nodded, tears running down my cheeks. I couldn't speak.

"The reason you need something stable and solid...is that"—he saw the look of panic in my eyes—"no, no, it's okay. I'm not going to ask. Just—is that because of something in your past? Something you don't want to talk about?"

I nodded. I could feel myself tensing up, but it wasn't as bad as it had been when we'd been out on the driveway. I was emotionally exhausted, incapable of getting angry with him, and he was looking at me with such sadness it broke my heart.

"It holds the memories back," I said at last. "Stops me sliding down into them. So does dancing. So does the bike."

He frowned. "The bike? Your exercise bike?"

I let out a snort of teary laughter, and nodded. "But none of it works as well as...you."

He moved off his seat, closing the gap between us. He looked me right in the eye and waited until I was completely, utterly focused on him, as if he wanted to be sure that his words would really soak in. "I'm not going anywhere," he told me.

I sniffed, blinking tears from my eyes, and slid off my seat. We met in the middle of the tub, and he wrapped his arms around me, pulling me to him, our clothes flapping and tangling in the water. He pushed my sopping hair back out of my face and laid kisses on my forehead, then down my cheek, and then we were clinging together, close enough to share heartbeats, warm and safe in the water as the rain hammered down outside.

"I don't know if I can stop," I told him haltingly.

"Okay," he said, and I knew he meant it. I knew he'd wait for me, for as long as it took—forever, if he had to. As he held me, the feel of his arms and the touch of his cheek nursed something back to life, deep inside me, a tiny glimmer I'd thought was gone forever: hope. If he could resist pushing, accept that there was a part of me he'd never know...maybe we still had a shot.

***

We stayed there for a full half hour, the water gradually warming us through. After a while, I slipped my dress off under the water and sat there in my bra and panties—I wasn't ready for naked, yet. He stripped down to his jockey shorts and we sat with my back against his chest, looking out at the rain as it pounded the ground, six feet away but unable to touch us.

When it became obvious that the rain wasn't going to stop, we agreed to make a dash for the house. We left our wet bundles of clothes by the side of the tub, scrambled out and ran in our underwear down the garden, the freezing rain sluicing down our steaming bodies. By the time we'd run around the side of the mansion and in through the front door, our feet were sticky with mud from the waterlogged lawn and we were gasping and shaking with cold. Without words, we headed straight upstairs to his bedroom and then through to the shower. We stood there under the spray, trying to stand so it could rain down on both of us, and watched the water blast away the mud until we were clean and perfect.

I looked up into his eyes and felt the mood change. The anger and hurt wasn't forgotten, but we had a fresh start.

And that left us standing near-naked in the shower.

He moved just fractionally closer to me, leaning in over me and blocking the spray with his body. I could feel everything speed up as the realization of what was going to happen hit us both at the same time.

He leaned down and kissed me, lips just brushing at first as I raised my head to him. Then tasting, his hands on my shoulders and the wet straps of my bra. It felt like we were kissing for the first time—a whole new part of me had opened up to him, and as ugly and broken as it was, he loved all of me. He moved back a little, checking it was okay. Waiting for a sign.

I reached back and unhooked my bra, then peeled it off and let it fall with a wet slap of fabric. Then his body was against mine, my breasts mashing against his chest as he drove me back against the wall. His mouth was at my throat, kissing the water from my skin as he worked his way down to my shoulder, to that magical bit of skin along my collarbone where his lips made me go weak.

My hands were on his back, tracing the hard contours of his muscles. As his hands cupped my breasts, mine were sliding down his back and around to the side. One palm felt the ridges of his scars and he drew back again, looking into my eyes. I tensed, thinking he was about to push my hand away....

He put his own hand over mine and held it in place. I nodded and held him close, my body molding to his, my lips against his chest.

Then he gently moved back and started to kneel down in front of me. I had to clench my fists to keep from stopping him, feeling his eyes track down my stomach, down to my thighs. The hot wave of shame as he saw my scars close up. He moved forward and kissed them, a feather touch against the brutal lines, and I had to bite my lip to let him do it, force myself not to turn away. He kissed them again and again, and with each kiss the hot shame lifted just a little, until finally I could accept his eyes there, his touch there.

He felt me relax, and his mouth moved away from me. A second later, his hands hooked under my sodden panties and peeled them down and off my legs. Then my shoulders were pressing hard against the tiles as his lips and tongue found me, his shoulders nudging my legs wider as he began long, long minutes of licking and plunging and circling until I turned my face up into the spray, eyes squeezed tight shut, and gasped and panted into the water as I came.

I stood under the spray as he went over to the bathroom cabinet. Through the steam I saw him roll on a condom, and then we was back in front of me, moving between my thighs, and I kissed him hungrily as he drove up into me, his hands on my ass. I felt myself lifted and wrapped my legs around him. He took each nipple in turn into the slick heat of his mouth, letting the spray lash the other one, until I ground and panted against him. He started to move inside me, pinning me to the wall as he thrust, long glorious strokes that made the heat within me spin faster and faster. I dug my fingers hard into his shoulders, writhed and trembled and finally, as we both reached our peaks, I called out his name.

CHAPTER THIRTY-ONE

Darrell

I WOKE UP SWEATING AND GASPING, the hot desert air still in my lungs. She was asleep next to me, naked—I'd managed to pull the sheets off both of us during my nightmare and she was sleepily protesting at the sudden cold.

I allowed myself one long look at her body's smooth perfection and then covered her up and sat there for a while, until I was sure she was fully asleep. Then I pulled on some jeans and padded downstairs. I could feel the rage building up inside, but I'd long ago learned how to clamp down on it until I reached the workshop.

When I was safely down there, I turned the music up loud, pulled the sheet off the missile and went to work. I could hear the screams in my head even over the music and smell the sickly scents of the burning wreckage. I moved faster and faster, my fingers barely able to keep up with my brain's commands. I'd been a fool to even think about going against this, to fight with Carol. However much I loved Natasha, it didn't change a damn thing that had happened. Mom and Dad were still dead, and I wasn't going to forget them. I had a job to do.

I'd finally figured it out, the strength of the nightmare forcing my brain to make that last, vital connection. I could see it, as clearly as if I'd already built it. The missile's internal parts, even its fuel tanks, strung on cables so they could move inside it, allowing it to shift its weight. It would be able to curve and dodge in the air as gracefully as a bird—as gracefully as *her*.

I thought of her as I worked, and she did a better job than the music or the physical work at pushing the memories back. I'd almost driven her away, with my questions and my need to understand everything, to fix everything. I knew now she was running from something in her past, something that maybe, eventually, she could share with me. Maybe we weren't so different. I could have easily wound up clinging on to self-harming, or alcohol, or something equally bad. I'd been lucky that I'd found this way of venting my anger—

I froze.

Had I, though? Had I really been lucky? Natasha only hurt herself. How many was I hurting, every time I built something? How many would this new creation kill?

I killed the music and stood there staring at the missile. A month before, I would have been proud of it, reveled in its brutal efficiency. Now it made me sick. I was creating something that couldn't be undone, something that would destroy cities, orphan children. I was twenty-four and my entire career to date had been spent making things that killed. Was this going to be my life?

Carol's words in my head. *You're a hero.*

Was I? Suddenly, I wasn't so sure.

CHAPTER THIRTY-TWO

Natasha

I WOKE NAKED AND ALONE IN HIS BED, the pre-dawn light making the curtains glow. I reached out a hand and the sheets where he'd lain were cold. He'd been gone for hours.

My underwear was a sodden pile on the bathroom floor and my dress was out by the hot tub. I wrapped a sheet around me instead and crept downstairs, blinking myself gradually awake. He wasn't in the kitchen making a snack, or in the lounge watching TV. He wouldn't leave without saying something...would he?

Then I saw the elevator door. The indicator above it showed that the lift was down at the workshop. I sighed. The work, again—in the middle of the night? I thought about leaving him to it. I didn't want to seem like I was trying to possess him, and I knew that this was how he lived. I'd been angry when he'd tried to stop me cutting. What right did I have to stop him working, especially if—as I suspected—throwing himself into his work was his way of coping with his demons?

But he'd tried to help me, and I should try to help him. Wasn't it the duty of the wife or girlfriend to drag her man to bed when he pushed himself too hard?

I rode the elevator down, the trip underground weirdly claustrophobic without him. When the doors opened, he was still in the process of throwing a sheet over his mystery creation. I got just a glimpse of something smooth and white.

"Hi." He sounded abashed. "Sorry. Did I wake you?"

I shook my head. "No, but...it's nearly morning. How long have you been down here?"

He looked at his feet. "I don't know. A while." He sighed. "Sometimes I can't sleep, you know?" He looked exhausted, and somehow lost.

I knew then that I'd been right—the work was his way of escaping from whatever his dreams unearthed. "Do you want to talk about it?"

I saw him hesitate, and held my breath. But he shook his head. "I can't. I'm sorry."

I nodded and held out my hand. "Come back to bed."

He shook his head. "I'll just toss and turn and disturb you. I don't think I could sleep right now. You go ahead." And he turned away.

I was new to the girlfriend thing, but I was pretty sure what I was meant to do at that point. I let go of the sheet and felt it unwind from my body, dropping to the floor with a soft rustle of fabric. He turned at the sound and gaped at me.

"I didn't say you had to sleep," I told him, and held out my hand again. This time, he took it.

***

Back upstairs, it was languid and tender, his body like rock beneath me as I straddled him, his hands on my breasts as he drove his hips up into me.

When I woke again, it was morning and this time he was sleeping soundly, my head on his chest. I lay there for a while, enjoying the moment, but eventually my growling stomach nudged me in the direction of coffee and food. Fortunately I'd thought to leave my panties on the heated towel rail in the bathroom when we'd come back upstairs, and they were just about dry. I teamed them with one of Darrell's t-shirts, and while the result wasn't exactly fashionable, it was better than walking around naked.

Downstairs, the morning light was blasting through the windows: when we'd dashed inside, we'd been in too much of a hurry to lower the blinds. I winced at the muddy footprints that led from the front door up the stairs.

In the kitchen, I fumbled around for milk and mugs and figured out the coffee machine, then discovered there was no coffee left. I sighed and rested my forehead against the cupboard door, remembering using the last of it. I needed coffee. I had the second audition at two that afternoon, and classes before that. I had to find something dry to wear, say goodbye to Darrell and get back into the city, fast. The thought of doing all that in my current sleepy state didn't bear thinking about.

Then I remembered the coffee pot down in the workshop and sighed in relief. I'd make a couple of mugs and we could drink it while we waited for a cab.

I took the milk and mugs downstairs and—yes!— there was coffee. I waited for the machine to do its thing, yawning and glancing idly around. It was a few minutes before my eyes fell on Darrell's project, hidden beneath its sheet.

CHAPTER THIRTY-THREE

Darrell

I'LL NEVER BE SURE WHAT WOKE ME. I'd been in the soundest sleep I'd enjoyed for years, Natasha's head cradled on my chest. And then suddenly, something was wrong and I was struggling back up to consciousness, my brain still fuddled. She wasn't there. Okay, no big deal—it looked like it was morning. So why did I feel so unsettled?

The bathroom was empty. I pulled my jeans back on and headed downstairs, calling her name. Had she left already, rushing back to Fenbrook for classes? Wouldn't she have woken me, or at least left a note?

In the kitchen I saw the cupboard open, the coffee machine standing ready but unused. Why had she—

God, *no*.

I rushed back into the hallway. We'd taken the elevator back up just a few hours ago, so it should have been right there on the ground floor. But however much I willed it, the indicator above the door said it was down at the workshop.

I thumped the elevator button as hard as I could, as if that would make it come faster.

CHAPTER THIRTY-FOUR

Natasha

IT SEEMED TO DRAW ME TO IT. Partly it was that outburst of Carol's—I needed to understand what had happened between them to make her so angry. Partly it was jealousy. I knew he struggled to put anything, including me, ahead of his work. What was it that had him so deeply ensnared, and why did he choose it, and not drugs or sex or one of a million other things, to escape into? And partly it was just wanting to see what he did—he got to see my work every day, but aside from the whiteboard I'd never seen the results of his efforts.

I figured I'd take a look and never tell him. A little voice inside me whispered that maybe that's exactly what he'd thought, when he'd opened the cigarette case. But I squashed that voice—it was just his *work,* for God's sake. It wasn't some deep dark secret. How bad could it be?

I was trying to work out what it was as I approached, and some of my curiosity was because I knew that it was inspired by me—however crazy that sounded.

I tried to think about all the things that a highly-paid designer might design. A car? I'd heard of car designers being inspired by nature and animals. A car inspired by a woman—by how a dancer moved—didn't sound completely nuts, although I had visions of him pointing to flaring wheel arches, telling me they were based on my hips, and me slapping him. But the thing only looked to be about eight feet long—too small for a car.

Suddenly it clicked. *A motorbike!* Of course—he was into bikes, after all. I'd seen the Ducati parked outside the mansion, that first time I'd visited. He'd built some sort of super-fast sports bike. And weren't bikes all about leaning into corners and using your weight to stabilize you? That would make perfect sense.

I smiled to myself. I had a boyfriend who designed cool motorbikes. Maybe he'd take me for a ride on it, when it was finished. Then I caught my breath. Maybe he'd even name it after me! Every dancer knows the story of Ana Pavlova, and how a chef named the dessert after her.

My hand was already lifting the sheet to confirm my guess when I heard the elevator doors open behind me.

"Natasha, no!"

I turned to smile at him and was amazed at how worried he looked. Perhaps he didn't want me to see it before it was finished, like an artist with a portrait. My smile widened. How like him, to want everything to be perfect. *It's okay,* I started to say, *I know what it is.*

I turned back to the thing as the sheet slid off.

***

When I was six, my dad had taken me on a

backwoods hike with the aim of seeing some nature. We'd seen precisely nothing for about three hours and then, just as we were walking back to the car, he'd pointed something out in the sky. A hawk, wheeling and circling effortlessly, heartbreakingly beautiful, its feathers gleaming in the late afternoon sun. And then it had dived with astonishing speed and skimmed the ground not twenty feet from us, and as it rose it had some tiny, helpless animal in its beak, still twitching as it was carried aloft. I'd cried, while my Dad had tried to explain to me about *nature, red in tooth and claw*.

Now, looking at the thing Darrell had built, I got the same feeling. It was beautiful and utterly horrific.

The casing was snow white and glossy, and every surface on the long body seemed to be a precise, flowing curve leading to the fins at the back. The side of the thing was open, and inside was what looked like the wires of a piano, stretched taut and shining along its length, with gleaming black cylinders strung along them like an abacus. More cylinders were stacked on the floor—he'd been working on that part, I realized, when I dragged him back to bed.

Darrell came to stand behind me. His hands settled on my arms, but my body was tense and unyielding under his touch.

"Tell me it's something else," I said.

He stayed silent, and I swallowed.

"It's only for defense. Right? One of those missiles that shoots down other missiles." My voice was thin and strained, almost lost in the huge room.

He didn't speak, didn't even shake his head. He just rested his brow against the back of my head. I wanted to understand. I wanted to find a way for it to be okay.

"What does it do?" I swallowed. "What does

it...destroy?"

He took a deep breath and then let it out. When he spoke, it sounded like each word cut him like a knife. "The nose cone is designed to hold a 300 kiloton warhead."

I'd heard that word *kiloton* on old war documentaries. I knew what it meant, but I had to be sure. "What will that do?"

He swallowed. "Destroy a city. This is one of six— we call them MIRVs—that sit inside a...." He broke off and sighed. I knew, somehow, that he'd closed his eyes behind me, unable to look anymore. "Six of these will eventually sit inside the main missile. Six cities."

I was shaking. I didn't know when I'd started, but I couldn't stop. "Tell me...tell me there's none of *me* in there." I tried to swallow. "Tell me you're working on something else as well. Tell me—" I could feel myself starting to cry, and broke off.

He walked around me and stood next to it, the scientist next to his monster. In his eyes, I could see how much pain this was causing him, but I could see he was desperate to give me the truth, too. He pointed to the guts of it, the black cylinders on their piano wires. "I made it able to shift its weight. It can twist by pulling all the weight suddenly to one side, or change course by pulling all the weight forward or back."

"Just like me," I said tightly.

He nodded.

I could feel tears rolling down my cheeks and balled my hands into fists, because I didn't want him to see me cry. I wanted to be strong, dammit. I wanted him to know how angry I was.

"I don't..." I shook my head. "I don't want to be part of...*this.*"

He put his hands up in defense. "I didn't mean to

hurt you—"

"You *lied* to me. You got me in here to dance and the whole time you were building *this*." I shook my head. "What did you think my reaction was going to be?" I was rewinding in my head through everything that had happened. "This is where all the money comes from? This is what Carol and you fought over?" Suddenly the peacenik comment made sense. "She thought I knew, didn't she? She thought I was dragging you away from it."

"We fought because I was having doubts. Ever since you came along." His voice was tight now, growing angry. He'd stepped between me and the missile, as if to protect it.

"Well, they didn't stop you, did they?" I could hear the bitterness in my voice and hated it, but at that moment, I hated him for lying to me even more.

"It's not that simple."

I thought I'd misheard. "Yes it *is*, Darrell! God...yes it *is!* Building this stuff, thinking up ways to destroy cities—yes, that's *wrong!* Why is that even a question for you?"

"It isn't. That. Simple." He grated the words out. I could see that vicious anger that I'd glimpsed when he'd had his nightmare clawing its way to the surface, but I was past caring.

"Then tell me!" I was still crying, but the tears were silent and cold now, frozen by the fear that I was about to lose him forever. Because after this, I didn't see how we could possibly go on. "Tell me! Tell me your *good reason* for doing this!"

And so, head down and his black hair flopping over his eyes, he told me. He told me about the day he'd watched his parents die. He told me about coming back to the US and embarking on his path of revenge, building something to strike back at the people who'd ripped his mom and dad from him. He told me about Carol, about how she'd told him he was doing the right thing and encouraged him to continue after that first time. She'd even helped him choose the mansion and arranged the contractors to build his workshop.

I stood there listening in growing horror. There were very few people I actually hated, but this woman who'd used and corrupted him, forced his growth in a direction that suited her...I hated her more than anyone I'd ever known.

When I'd demanded an explanation, I hadn't thought there was anything he could say that would justify what he'd done. I just wanted to hear his side of it—I figured I owed him that. But as he told me, I *did* understand. I could see exactly why he'd done it. I just had no idea if I could save him.

When he'd finished, we both stood there in silence for a moment. I knew I had to choose my words carefully, even as I reeled in shock. "Darrell...I'm sorry."

He nodded. I could see he was trying not to cry. I'd just forced him to relive it all.

"But...." I stepped in close and put my hands on his chest. "Darrell, you have to see, she's using you. She should never have let you get into this."

"It was my choice. I went to her with my first design." A defensive note in his voice.

"You were nineteen! And in the middle of grieving! She should have made you get help—counseling, something."

He shook his head. "She said that wouldn't help."

Hate for this woman was bubbling up inside me like boiling tar. She'd taken this perfect, loving man and made him live in misery and barely repressed rage for four years, just so she could get rich. "She's using you," I said again. "Darrell, you have to see that. Maybe the first time—I don't know—maybe that was okay, maybe you needed to take revenge. But *this*"—I indicated the missile—"this has nothing to do with your parents. It has nothing to do with the Middle East and terrorists. This is for wiping out another country!"

He just stared at me, and for once, those beautiful eyes weren't clear and honest. They were clouded by something. By her. "I can't," he told me. "I can't just walk away. I thought maybe I could, but I can't."

I was going out of my mind. I could see how tightly she'd ensnared him, and I didn't know how to cut him free. "*Why?*"

His eyes were brimming with tears. "I can't forget about them."

I threw my arms around him. "You wouldn't be forgetting about them! Darrell, you wouldn't be—there are other ways, there are better ways of remembering them!"

He wasn't hugging me back. "You don't understand. If I don't do this—if I don't work every hour I can—it's like I don't...." He sighed. "You wouldn't understand."

And then I knew. The realization was like being on the downward plunge of a rollercoaster, my stomach dropping a million feet as I saw how I could save him. There was only one way to connect with him, one way to let him know he wasn't alone in his pain.

God, not that. Please not that.

But I could see him turning inward, closing down. I only had this one chance to make him see.

"I do understand," I said very quietly. "There's something I need to tell you."

Helena Newbury

CHAPTER THIRTY-FIVE

Natasha
Six years earlier

MOM GETS ME TO RECITE her cell number for like the eightieth time and Dad makes me promise to get to bed by ten because it's a school night tomorrow. I wait until I hear their car leave the drive, then give it another five minutes—just to be sure. Mom said they'd be back by midnight. It's eight-thirty—I have half an hour before he gets here.

I get out of the jeans and t-shirt I was wearing and into the dress I bought secretly and snuck home from the mall. Black, with a scoop neck and a short skirt. If Mom saw it she'd say it was *a little too daring for fifteen* and Dad would never let me leave the house. Not that I have any intention of leaving the house tonight.

Craig's coming over.

I have to go to the bathroom to do my make-up. I don't have a mirror in my room, because I'm camped out in the den downstairs while Dad lays a new floor in my real bedroom—a job he started a week ago and still hasn't quite figured out how to finish. I love him, but sometimes I just wish he'd admit his shortcomings and hire a handyman.

I'm quick, because I've been planning exactly what I'm going to do for days. Heck, I've been planning the whole night for days. I carefully paint dark lips and artfully smudged grey eye shadow. I wish my hair was black but apart from that, I figure I carry the goth look off pretty well. Craig's going to love it.

I run through to the lounge to start getting stuff ready. I've bought some long lengths of black silk from a fabric shop. Well, I'd wanted silk, but silk was seriously expensive. This stuff looks cheap and ragged-edged, but I'm hoping it'll look better when I turn the lights out. I use tape to fix it to the walls, because thumbtacks would mark the wallpaper. Soon it hangs in long, graceful curves overhead, making the place look like some sort of Bedouin tent.

I get out the candles and just go mental with them, putting them all around the edges of the room, on the table, on the windowsills.... By the time I get them all lit it's just after nine, but the room looks amazing. Everything's in flickering, romantic half-shadow, and when I check myself in the mirror it totally hides the couple of pimples I was worried about. Craig's not going to be able to resist me. I think tonight might be the night we finally do it. I'm so excited I actually have to resist clapping my hands together. I'm ready! Then one of the candles goes out and the little coil of smoke sets the smoke alarm off, so I have to climb up on a chair and yank the battery. OK...*now* I'm ready.

It's been slow and gentle so far with him. We've been dating for three weeks, but it's sooo hard to get time alone together, with both sets of parents watching us like hawks. Thank God for Dad's company party tonight. I swear, it's the only night they actually go out each year.

I hear his knock at the door just as I remember the finishing touch—the bottle of vodka some guy at work gave Dad. I am grounded like *forever* if he finds out, but that bottle's been sitting there half-empty for over a year. I figure that if we only have a little bit and top it up with water, he'll never know.

I answer the door and Craig's standing there grinning, tight black t-shirt over his whipcord body. The guy barely eats—part of the whole goth thing, I guess—but he's cute as hell and smart and funny. I can feel my heart racing, every moment of my life up to now fading away into insignificance. *Tonight is the night!*

I throw some cushions down on the floor and we lie there in the candlelight, laughing and talking and occasionally kissing. I try some vodka and *Jeez* it burns. How do people drink this stuff? But I feel all warm and mellow inside, so I drink a little more. The talking dies away and there's more kissing and more vodka and I'm seriously thinking that tonight it's going to happen when I hear the sound I really don't want to hear: car tires on gravel.

I check the clock. *Shit!* It's ten after midnight! I grab Craig and push him towards the back door, then run around blowing out all the candles. I realize I'm a little drunk—how much vodka did we drink, anyway? The adrenaline helps me focus. If they find out Craig's been here without them knowing, *grounded* won't begin to cover it. There's no time to deal with the fabric so I just close the door. I lock the back door behind Craig and sprint for my temporary room in the downstairs den. I get there just as I hear Mom's key in the front door. As I peel off my dress and hide it under the covers, they're moving through the hall. I know Dad's had one glass of wine too many, because Mom's voice is patiently patronizing as she urges him along. There'll be teasing at the breakfast table tomorrow.

Please don't go in the lounge!

But they don't. It sounds like they're heading straight down the hall to the stairs. I pull on a nightshirt and slip quietly under the covers. When one of them—I think it's Mom—cracks open the door and peeks in, I'm doing a pretty good impression of sleeping.

I hear my door close, and then they're moving up the stairs to bed. *Whew.*

All I have to do now is wait for them to go to sleep, then creep back into the lounge, gather everything up and hide it away. I'll refill Dad's vodka bottle with water and no one will ever know. I got away with it! I lie there in the darkness, the memory of Craig's lips on mine making me grin, counting the minutes until it's safe to—

....

As my eyes open, the room looks weird...wrong. Lighter than it should, like someone's left the hall light on, except the glow isn't white: it's orange.

I sit up and the room spins. I can't breathe. I can barely see. I try to get up and stumble, and wind up on my hands and knees. It's easier to see down there, for some reason, and now I can see the orange glow coming from under the door and hear the rushing, roaring noise that finally connects in my half-drunk brain to *fire*.

I grab the metal doorknob and scream as I burn my hand. I cough and once I start, I can't stop. Air. I have to get air.

It takes whole minutes for my fumbling hands to free the window catch and then I swing it wide and I'm drinking in huge gulps of cool outside air. It rouses me enough that I manage to haul myself out of the window and drop to the grass outside. When I get to my feet and turn around, I see the flames roaring through the lounge window.

I stagger to the neighbor's house and hammer on the door until they wake up. It's an old couple, and the wife hugs me while he rings the fire service. Then he tries, despite his wife's protests, to smash his way in through the back door and get upstairs, but the flames are too fierce.

I keep thinking I'll hear them screaming, but there's nothing at all, no movement from the upstairs window.

***

A woman with blonde hair who smells of out-of-date perfume says she's from something called child services and asks me to go with her. She puts me to bed on a couch in a small office with horrible green wallpaper, but I don't sleep.

I wait for there to be questions, but there are none. Eventually the child services lady sits me down and tells me what happened: my parents, after they got home from the party, went into the lounge and sat around drinking vodka—they know this, because there were two glasses. They'd lit some candles and they must have left one of them burning, and for some reason they took the battery out of the smoke alarm.

That's not what happened, I want to say, *that's not what happened at all.* But she hugs me close as I start to cry and I can't seem to find my voice.

I don't see Craig for a week. We never speak again.

I'm introduced to Mr. and Mrs. Patterson, a nice foster couple. They've done this before, their previous foster child having just left for college, and their house seems nice. But it's not my house, and they're not my parents.

Is there anything you like to do? Mrs. Patterson asks me. She has a round face like a moon.

Dance, I tell her. *I go to dance lessons on Tuesdays and Thursdays and Saturdays.* And when they find out how much dance lessons cost, I can see there's some hesitation, but they have muttered conversations they think I can't hear, saying things like *it's the one thing she has left.* And I dance like I've never danced before, because maybe, if I dance and I dance and I dance, if I dance until my legs ache and my feet bleed, maybe I can punish myself enough.

CHAPTER THIRTY-SIX

Natasha

I STOPPED. There was more to tell: how I'd won a scholarship to Fenbrook, *"She's so committed! We've never seen a student with such focus!";* how I'd discovered cutting when I was nineteen, the dancing no longer seeming to work as well. But I seemed to run out of energy. After years of fearing I'd slip and slide down into those memories, I'd sunk down in them willingly, to save him, and now I was just...numb.

He was staring into my eyes, his face wracked with pain.

"Say something," I said.

He shook his head.

"I understand!" I told him. "I know what it's like to have it hanging over you, and it's fucked me up too, just in a different way. Come with me, away from all this!"

He looked at me for a long time. And then he finally said, in a voice dragged from his very soul, "I can't. I'm sorry. I can't."

And it was over.

We stared at each other for a moment, and then I turned around and walked to the elevator, knowing that I'd never see him again. Upstairs, I found the bag that I'd left out in the garden all night. My phone was soaked and ruined, but the cigarette case was just fine.

I found an old pair of his jeans and pulled them on, threw my wet clothes in my bag and called a cab. It was a beautiful, sun-drenched morning and all I wanted to do was curl up somewhere and die.

***

I had classes, but I didn't go. I didn't even call in sick. I had the cab stop at a drugstore and bought some fresh blades and dressings. I never normally bought the two things together, in case the salesperson got suspicious, but I was done hiding.

I wasn't crying. Maybe I was all cried out, but it felt more like I'd slipped off the tightrope I'd been walking for six years, the one the cutting and the bike and the dancing had helped me balance on. I'd fallen down into the cold, thick ocean of guilt and I was slowly drowning in it.

In my bedroom, I sat with the shining blades arranged in a row down my leg.

My hands were shaking as I cut, and I waited for the burn of punishment to calm them, but it didn't.

He hated me.

The second cut was no better, the line ragged and messy.

The best thing that had ever happened to me had been ripped away by the worst thing I'd ever done. In some tiny part of me, there was actually relief. I didn't need to try to be normal anymore. I'd had it confirmed to me that I was broken beyond repair, that even someone who loved me as much as Darrell had would abandon me in disgust as soon as they knew the truth.

The third cut hurt more, but not in the right way. It didn't lift me out of the swamp of memories, and I was sinking fast. Hot tears splashed salty pain into the wound—I hadn't even realized I'd started crying. I slapped a dressing over my thigh and climbed onto the bike, not even bothering to get changed. I cranked it up to maximum resistance and started pedaling, feeling the sweat burn into the cuts and my muscles ache like fire, but the tears kept coming, heavy and fast.

Clarissa found me like that an hour later, my legs still pumping at the pedals, the flywheel making an unearthly howl as I pushed it and myself past endurance. She had to pull me off it, and I beat on her back with my fists as I sobbed.

CHAPTER THIRTY-SEVEN

Darrell

I WAS KNEELING NEXT TO THE MISSILE, making the final adjustments. I'd turned the music up ear-splittingly loud, but it wasn't working anymore to drown out my memories.

I understood it all, now. She was punishing herself every day because she looked in the mirror and saw a murderer. She'd been living with guilt for six years, when she should have been getting help. She'd never been able to grieve, because she didn't think she deserved to.

And I couldn't help her.

I knew she'd told me to make me understand, to let me know that she was going through something similar. We were both trapped by our memories. And that's why, even though I longed to help her, I knew I couldn't. I knew I could never let them go. I could never give up on their memory and move on—it would be like forgetting them. I couldn't betray them like that. And if I couldn't do it myself, how could I expect her to?

She was better off without me.

The doubts I'd had before had solidified into a cold understanding. I'd worried that what I was doing was wrong. Natasha had made me sure of it, hoping that once I realized that, I'd break away from it. She hadn't realized just how strongly bound I was to my path—I knew now I was evil, but that didn't mean I could stop doing it. It just meant I now hated myself as much as I hated the men who'd killed my parents. Well, fine. If that's what it took to honor their memory, so be it.

The elevator chimed. I was didn't have to turn to see who it was. There was only one other person with a key to the house.

"I brought you a care package," Carol shouted over the music. Then, as she always did, she turned it off so that I'd have no choice but to speak to her. I sighed and turned around.

She was holding a crate of Dr. Pepper and two boxes of Krispy Kremes. I knew that one box would be all frosted, one all lemon meringue. Exactly what I liked.

"I wasn't happy about the way we left things," she told me sadly. "I wanted to check you were okay."

"Me, or the missile?" I was surprised by how much bitterness came through in my voice.

She did a good job of sounding shocked. "Darrell! You know how much I care about you. I knew you were...conflicted."

I shook my head and turned back to the missile. "I'm not anymore."

She watched me for a second. "You broke up?" She was unable to stop just a hint of relief creeping into her voice.

I nodded.

She came closer, crouched down and put her arms around me. I knelt there rigidly, not relaxing into it but not pulling away, either. "Oh, darling. God, that's awful. I know it's tough. But I think in the long term, it's for the best."

I gave a kind of half nod. "I'd like to be alone, now," I told her.

"Of course." She started to retreat, her heels clicking on the concrete.

"One thing," I said suddenly, without turning around.

"Anything, what?"

"Find me another project," I told her. "And...find someone to dismantle the stage."

"Consider it done."

When she'd gone, I turned back to the missile. I'd done everything I could usefully do, now, and was just making busy work. I started cleaning the casing, getting rid of all the oily finger marks and buffing it until it shone. But in the reflections, I kept glimpsing Natasha, as if she was dancing on the stage behind me.

I'd thought I could fix her. I'd thought I was dealing with some trauma from the past, like mine, and maybe I could have helped her with that. But she was facing her trauma again every day, every time she looked in the mirror. She thought she'd killed her parents, and she'd thought that every single day since she was fifteen. No wonder she cut herself. She'd claimed she'd been coping—and maybe she had—but I'd come in and ripped away her only way of dealing with things, making her feel ashamed of it. I'd wanted to know her secrets, and I'd cruelly torn her open to get them. And then she'd spilled her last, dark secret to try to help me, only to discover I was too far gone to save.

And now what would happen to her? Would she meet someone else, someone normal, who'd be able to help her break free of her past? I tried to tell myself it was true, but I knew in my gut that it wasn't. Ours had been a chance meeting, and she'd trusted me—probably against her instincts. Thanks to me, she wouldn't trust again for a long time—maybe never. I loved her, and I'd managed to leave her far worse than I'd found her.

What do you do when you realize you're the bad guy?

I pushed the thought out of my head. There was nothing I could do about it. She'd never accept me doing what I did, and there was no way I could quit. I was locked on this path.

I called a hire company and arranged for them to drop off a van in an hour. I'd drive the missile down to Virginia myself, delivering it to Carol's company personally—a road trip was just what I needed. When I got back, the stage would be gone and I could get on with whatever project Carol found for me next. Life could get back to normal and, in time, I could forget all about her. It was time to accept what I was and get on with it. That's what grown-ups did.

I called Neil and asked him if he'd skip classes at MIT for a couple of days to come with me. We could share the driving, put the bikes in the back of the van and ride back on them when we'd dropped off the missile. He could tell something was wrong, but he agreed to come, never able to pass up a long ride.

When he showed up, his first question was if Natasha was coming, too. He had a plan to pick up Clarissa and the girls could ride pillion on the way back, with us all camping in the forest. He even had a tent we could use.

I just looked at him, and he could see it in my eyes. His face fell, and he pulled me into one of his bone-crushing man hugs.

"What happened?" he asked, when he let me go.

I knew there was no way to explain. "I don't want to talk about it."

He gave me a long look. "It was the work, wasn't it? The goddamn work—"

"Just...." I shook my head. "No more distractions, from now on."

"*Distractions?* That *distraction* was the best thing that ever happened to you."

"Enough!" I almost yelled it, and the sudden flare of anger and hurt I saw in Neil's face made me cringe inside. What had I turned into?

It was late morning before we had Neil's Harley and my Ducatti strapped down in the back of the hired van, and slid the missile in between them. I didn't miss the disgusted looks Neil gave the thing. He'd tied his hair back in a bandana while we worked, and between that and his biker clothes he looked like someone the cops would pull over on the flimsiest excuse—indeed, that happened on a weekly basis and Neil took great pleasure in flashing his MIT ID card along with his license. He'd be a doctor of science pretty soon, and he chose to hang around with criminals and dress like an outlaw. He needed to grow up.

I started the engine, and then just sat there, my fingers tracing the steering wheel.

What if Neil wasn't the one who needed to grow up?

I was doing what I was supposed to do. It was what being an adult was all about: making the difficult choice instead of the easy one. Sacrificing what you wanted and doing what you needed.

Except....

What if this *was* the easy choice? I'd thought I was being brave, continuing on this path. But the thing that really scared me was changing course. If I stopped making weapons, I had literally no idea what the hell to do tomorrow, let alone the rest of my life. Even worse, I'd be admitting to myself that the last four years had been a mistake—that I'd been on the wrong path all along. What if Natasha was right, and there were better ways of remembering my folks? What if the really brave thing was to have the guts to let go of my past and make a fresh start...with someone I wanted to be with?

What if being an adult really came down to making my own decisions, instead of letting someone make them for me?

It was like a dam bursting open inside me, a tiny hole ripped wider and wider by the pressure. As the wall fell, I finally felt the certainty I'd been missing, the knowledge that this was *right*. And with it came a flipside, a sickening realization that everything I'd been doing since my parent's death had been wrong.

I had to fix everything. Fortunately, solving problems is what I do.

I turned to Neil. "Call Big Earl."

"Big-Earl-who-you-don't-approve-of, Big Earl?

"We need his help."

Neil looked over his shoulder at the missile. "We aren't going to Virginia?" he asked hopefully.

"We're not going to Virginia."

"Where are we going?"

"Fenbrook."

CHAPTER THIRTY-EIGHT

Natasha

CLARISSA SOMEHOW CAJOLED ME into the shower and then into some fresh clothes. She hugged and empathized and occasionally wished horrible deaths on Darrell, as if this was just your typical break up, but we both knew it wasn't. I could see the worry in her eyes, and she could see I wasn't just upset. I was broken, maybe in a way that could never be fixed.

We'd already missed one class and were late for the second, drawing glares from Miss Kay as we crept in. I tried to fill my mind with dance, but it didn't work. I felt raw and torn, the part of my heart that belonged to Darrell viciously ripped away. I kept missing steps. I couldn't even balance, my muscles weak and my joints stiff. Miss Kay took about three seconds to notice.

"Man trouble?" she asked, in a voice low enough that only I could hear it.

"What?"

"Someone's messing with your brain, honey, and you might want to tell them to quit. 'Cause the way you're moving, right now? I ain't seen that since you were a first day freshman."

I took a deep breath, thinking of the cigarette case. I hadn't had time to duck into the restroom before the class started. I didn't even know if cutting would still work for me—it hadn't that morning. "I'm sorry. I'll be better tomorrow. I just need a little time."

"What you *need* is to get your shit together. You split with someone?" I looked up, aghast, but she could see the truth in my eyes. "Yeah, I figured." Her expression softened minutely. "I'm sorry, Natasha." She patted me just once on the shoulder, the closest thing to affection she'd ever shown me, and walked off to correct someone's fouetté.

I was barely holding it together. When you meet someone—when you meet *the* someone—you see yourself in a whole new light. I'd liked myself, when I'd been with him. I'd felt normal. Now I was back to being *me,* and it's difficult to describe just how awful the return was. Before, at least I hadn't fully realized what I'd been missing. I wished I'd never met him.

....

No. That wasn't true. Our relationship had broken me, but the happiness we'd had together, the way he'd made me feel...that had been worth it, a thousand times over. Maybe this was my punishment—one last glimpse of the life I could have had, if I'd done things differently six years ago, and then it was ripped away to ensure that I'd never again do anything as selfish as try to love someone.

I could barely concentrate as I moved to the center to try a combination Miss Kay was drilling us on. I went through the motions, but my body felt as if it was made of wax. I powered upward in a grand jeté, floated for a second—

There was a crash as the doors opened and for a second, I thought I'd completely lost it and was reliving the audition. *He* was standing in the doorway, panting as if he'd just run up the stairs.

I landed, staggering a little, my mouth hanging open. Miss Kay was already turning to the door.

"You'd better not be a boyfriend," she told Darrell as she stalked toward him. Then she glanced over her shoulder and saw my expression. "Oh, Lord." She glared at Darrell. "Now you're *really* in trouble."

"I need to speak to her," Darrell told her. He looked over at me, and his eyes weren't clouded anymore. They were as bright and clear as I'd ever seen them.

He took a step towards me and suddenly Miss Kay's right leg was straight out in front of her, the tip of her shoe prodding him in the waist. The room went utterly silent. Both her legs were like iron, with not a hint of a wobble. "Whoah, whoah, whoah, *whoah!*" she told him. "You're already in my bad books, but if you go disruptin' my class, you and me are gonna have a *conversation.*"

I started forward, but Clarissa's arm came up in front of me. She shot a questioning look at me and I hesitated. After the way he'd hurt me, did I really want to open myself up again?

I looked into those gorgeous blue eyes. Yes. Yes, I did, because what was the alternative? Close myself down for the rest of my life? I'd had my glimpse of a better life, a better *me*, and if there was even a slim possibility that could still be real, I had to be brave enough to reach for it.

I came up behind Miss Kay. Her foot was still

prodding Darrell's stomach, and she gave every sign of being able to keep it there for a week if need be. She didn't have to turn around to know it was me. "Is this man the reason your pas de chat looks like a pas de herd-of-goddamn-buffalo?"

I took a deep breath. "Yes ma'am."

She stared at him. "Cute."

I didn't know who was blushing more, Darrell or me.

Miss Kay finally lowered her leg. "Two minutes," she told us, and walked off, clapping her hands for a break. The rest of the class began to chatter behind me, but they kept their voices low. They wanted to hear.

I pushed Darrell out into the hallway. He looked at me, panicked by the time limit. I just nodded, trying to stop my lower lip from trembling. We had to do this here, now.

He closed his eyes for a second, getting it straight in his head. Then those clear blue eyes pinned me and he spread his hands wide. "I'm sorry. When you told me about what happened to you, I was caught up in my past. All I could think about was us splitting up, and how it was all my fault." His fingers gently stroked my cheek, and I caught my breath. "I was a selfish bastard. I should have made sure that even if we split up, I still told you...." He swallowed and I held my breath. "Natasha, it was *not your fault*. It was a horrible, horrible accident and it changed you forever but you don't need to carry this guilt around with you anymore. You were a kid and you made a mistake but their deaths were *not* your fault."

I realized that his hands were on my shoulders. I knew I should say something, but I couldn't speak. I'd been waiting six years for someone to say those words to me, while at the same time ensuring that no one ever could. It had taken my bid to save Darrell to let him save me.

All of my memories came rushing up out of the darkness, but for the first time it didn't feel like I was falling down into a pit. They were still raw and painful—in fact, I had the horrible realization that the dancing and the cutting and the bike meant I hadn't ever allowed myself to fully relive them—but I no longer felt like I was sliding out of control. I was terrified of them, but facing them seemed possible, now.

I drew in a deep, shuddering breath and nodded, seeing his relief through a film of tears. But I knew we weren't done. My past hadn't been the only thing that had ripped us apart. As long as his work and Carol still possessed him, there was no way we could be together. And if that hadn't changed, if he knew we were apart for good...my guts twisted. Did that mean he'd just lied about my past, safe in the knowledge that he'd never see me again? Was he just easing his conscience, and hated me after all?

I looked into his eyes and I couldn't see any deception there. I didn't believe he'd lie to me—not about that—but then I hadn't believed him capable of evil, either. How could I ever completely trust him, knowing what he did? Would Carol manipulate him into building more and worse weapons? And would she keep whispering in his ear until he slept with her?

"What about you?" Barely more than a whisper.

"I'll show you." He held out his hand. "If you'll come with me."

"Now?"

"Has to be right now. You'll see why."

It took a heartbeat to decide. I pushed back through the doors and Miss Kay was standing there waiting, hands on hips. The rest of the class stood silent and curious behind her.

I didn't have to say anything, my expression telling her everything she needed to know. She pursed her lips. "You'd better be in here early tomorrow with moves like I've never seen."

I nodded frantically and ran.

***

Downstairs, Neil was using every ounce of his charm to stop a female police officer slapping a ticket on a van. We got in, me in the middle, and sped off with him promising her good karma.

"Where are we going?" I asked as we headed out of the city. Looking behind my seat, I could see a long shape with a sheet thrown over it, and a sports bag. "Is that—"

"Yep. And we're going to Big Earl's," Darrell said.

From the look of raw determination on his face, Big Earl's wasn't somewhere anyone went willingly. It suddenly sank in that I was in a leotard and tights. "What are we going to do at Big Earl's?"

Darrell gave me a long look. "The right thing."

***

Big Earl's turned out to be a series of linked lots, surrounded by chain link fences topped with razor wire. There was a motorcycle club, a garage and a junkyard. Darrell parked the van outside the club, and six guys in biker gear sauntered over, menace on their faces. Neil jumped out and nodded to them, and that seemed to pacify them. Then I climbed out in my ballet gear and suddenly they were *very* interested.

Another car pulled up—a green Aston Martin. Carol got out, slammed her door and looked around her.

"What the hell, Darrell? I mean, really, what the hell?" She glanced at me, smirking at my outfit.

"Let's take a walk," Darrell told her coldly. Neil threw me his leather jacket and I slipped it on, and then Darrell was leading Carol and me through a gate into the junkyard, leaving Neil with the van.

The roads between the stacks of rusting cars were packed dirt, and my pointe shoes were trashed by the time I'd gone ten paces. Carol, in her Jimmy Choos, didn't fare much better. "An explanation, Darrell?" she said. "What is this—a new project? Please tell me you've arranged a demonstration."

"In a manner of speaking," Darrell told her. I'd never heard him sound so calm...or so cold.

It was a few minutes before we reached the end of the row. As we turned the corner, we heard a car roar up, and got there just in time to see Carol's Aston Martin screech to a stop, top down and Neil at the wheel.

Carol tensed, about to shout something, but then her eyes narrowed. As Neil got out and walked towards us, we saw the missile, wedged diagonally into the space behind the Aston's front seats. "It's finished?" Carol asked, suddenly breathless. "I can take it right now?"

"It's finished," Darrell told her. Then he looked at me. "But you aren't taking it."

A massive, four-wheeled loader roared up, with two vicious-looking forks pointing straight out in front. Everyone looked from it to the car, and Carol had time to draw in a single, strangled breath before the forks stabbed straight through the car's body and out the other side.

"*Are you insane?*" Carol's voice shook. "That's my—"

"Sabre gave it to me." Darrell reminded her. "I let you have it because I thought I owed you. But you've been using me from the start."

The loader heaved the car into the air and rolled forward. A few pieces of the Aston fell to the ground—a door mirror, a license plate—as if it was bleeding. Now everyone turned to look at where the loader was heading: the car crusher.

"You can't," Carol said, her face deathly pale. "Darrell, we've got buyers for the missile. You can't—" She started forward, but Neil clapped a firm hand on her shoulder.

"You shouldn't be worrying about the missile." Darrell was speaking to Carol, but looking at me. "In the trunk there's a bag. In the bag is every hard drive from every one of my computers. Everything I've ever made for you, for the last four years."

The loader dumped the car into the crusher and reversed away. A man—from his girth, Big Earl—stood ready at the crusher controls.

Carol spun to face Darrell. "That's your *work!* That's your *life's work!*"

Darrell took a deep breath. "That's not the life I want anymore." He looked at me. "Lift your hands above your head."

"What?" Everything was happening so fast.

"Lift your hands above your head." Darrell indicated the crusher. "It's the signal."

"*Don't!*" Carol's voice was like ice. She stepped in front of me, but somehow, despite her designer clothes and her perfect hair, I wasn't intimidated anymore.

I thought of the countless hours Darrell must have spent in that workshop. "Are you sure?"

He walked over and kissed me, his warm lips feeling so right on mine that I thought I was going to melt into the ground. He clutched me to him, one arm around my waist as with the other he stroked my pinned-back hair. After a second, I remembered to lift my arms above my head. I was too busy kissing him to see the car crushed, but I heard the tortured groan of metal and the popping as the windows broke. The most satisfying sound was Carol's utter, shocked silence as she realized she'd been beaten. When we finally broke the kiss, she was still staring at the crusher.

"What did you do to him?" she said at last, her voice raw and savage.

I gazed at Darrell. "I inspired him," I told her proudly.

As we walked back to the van, we kept casting little glances at each other. The wind was blowing his hair and he kept grinning every time he looked at me— and I knew I was doing the same. He was free. I didn't have to share him anymore, didn't have to see him eaten up from the inside by his rage. God knows we both still needed healing, but we'd taken the first steps. I felt whole, for the first time in six years.

We climbed into the van. I had my whole life ahead of me. My man, my friends, my career—

I suddenly looked at the clock on the dashboard. Twenty to two. I sat back in my seat and laughed.

Darrell climbed into the driver's seat. "What?"

I shook my head. "Nothing. Doesn't matter. I just—I had a call back today for the audition. The one you first saw me at."

"Well? Let's go!"

I smiled sadly at him. "It's back in the city and it starts in twenty minutes."

He looked over his shoulder at his bike, strapped down in the back of the van. "I can get you there in ten."

***

Three minutes later, I was clinging to Darrell's back as we roared around a corner, leaning so far over that my knees felt like they were brushing the highway. Neil had lent me his helmet and I'd kept on his leather jacket, but otherwise I was still in my ballet outfit. If I'd dared to lift my face from between Darrell's shoulders, I would have seen people giving us some very odd looks.

We whipped around an 18-wheeler, missing an oncoming SUV by scant inches. I wanted to scream, but I wasn't sure if it was in exhilaration or terror.

***

I burst through the door of the audition room and saw Sharon Barkell do a double take. I'd taken off the helmet, but I was still wearing a biker jacket and my pointe shoes were stained brown with mud.

"Is everything...are you alright?" she asked.

I walked to the center of the room. "Everything's just fine," I told her, beaming. Darrell crept in and I tossed him the helmet and jacket. He took a seat at the back, just like the first time.

I wasn't kidding myself. We both had a long way to go, and I knew that when the adrenaline wore off there would be more pain as we healed. But knowing that we'd face that together, it seemed possible. Anything seemed possible.

"Okay," said Sharon. "Same thing as last time, but with a little more lightness. Give me a second." She fiddled with her laptop, cueing up the music.

I looked across at Darrell. He'd done his part, but lifting the guilt from me was still only the first step. The next one I had to take on my own.

For the first time in a long, long time, I let go of everything. I let go of the feeling of the still-fresh cuts on my thigh. I let go of the feeling of my legs, aching from the punishment I'd given them on the bike. I even let go of Darrell—for a little while—and trusted that he'd be there when I needed him. As the music started, I allowed myself to just...*be,* stepping out with nothing to cling onto and accepting the memories for what they were. For once, I wasn't dancing to block something out or to punish myself. I was dancing for the sheer simple joy of it and there was nothing so good in the world.

Thank you for reading! If you enjoyed Dance For Me, please consider leaving a review.

If you'd like to know when I release a new book, you can join my mailing list here:
http://eepurl.com/zmvuH

You can also find me on my blog at:
http://helenanewbury.com

Or at:
https://twitter.com/HelenaAuthor
https://www.facebook.com/HelenaNewburyAuthor
http://www.goodreads.com/helenanewburyauthor
http://gplus.to/HelenaNewbury
http://pinterest.com/helenanewbury/

Or just drop me an email at:
helenanewburyauthor@gmail.com

Thanks again!
Helena

20212997R00152

Made in the USA
Charleston, SC
01 July 2013